Lorraine DeSousa was born in Cheshire, England in March 1960. This is the third book she has written and the first one she has submitted for publication. She has had a few poems published in small poetry anthologies. She now lives in The Algarve with her partner and her dogs.

For Carlos, Alex and Gaby with love.

Lorraine DeSousa

DELUSIONS

AUSTIN MACAULEY PUBLISHERS™

LONDON · CAMBRIDGE · NEW YORK · SHARJAH

A CIP catalogue record for this title is available from the British Library.

ISBN 9781398434417 (Paperback)
ISBN 9781398434424 (ePub e-book)

www.austinmacauley.com

First Published 2022
Austin Macauley Publishers Ltd®
1 Canada Square
Canary Wharf
London
E14 5AA

I would like to thank Fernando Miguel for his unending patience whilst I was writing, and the team at Austin Macaulay Publishers for helping me bring this book to fruition.

Prologue

Antigonish

William Hughes Mearns 1899

"Yesterday, upon the stair,
I met a man who wasn't there!
He wasn't there again today,
Oh, how I wish he'd go away!"

Her Voice

"Is all that we see or seem
But a dream within a dream?"
– Edgar Allen Poe

A man sits in a room, in front of him there is a clock. It ticks interminably slowly, seeming like a tock every hour instead of every second. The other strange thing about the clock is that the hands are moving anti-clockwise.

Besides the man sat on the chair, and the clock on the wall going backwards, there is nothing else in the room that we can see. As we look at the room further, we notice there is no door to the room, no way in and no way out. The walls and floor are made of grey stone slabs; the ceiling has one single light bulb hanging from the middle of the ceiling directly over the man's dark hair.

The man has no discernible features, nothing that would make him stand out in a crowd. He has on a flowered shirt and white shorts; it's as if he came from the beach. He is wearing flip flops and it seems like the air in the room must be cooler for him than his attire has allowed. We occasionally see him shiver as though there is a breeze in the room. But there is no breeze, no windows, no doors, nothing but the clock and the false light above his head.

Just a man on a wooden chair, watching a clock play lento with the passage of time.

That isn't to say though that the man does not move whilst we watch him. Occasionally, he will put his hand to his forehead and stroke his brow or he will cross then unfold his legs. This is almost in time with the clock's gradual tick. But other than the occasional movement, there is nothing else for him to do but sit and wait.

Wait for what you may ask? We do not know this; we can only observe him sitting, watching the slow clock and occasionally crossing and uncrossing his legs.

So many unanswered questions. Has he previously tried to escape from this room? Is that all he is, just a man sat in a room watching the passage of time?

Or is the end the beginning and the beginning the end?

His Voice

Be Happy for This Moment, This Moment Is Your Life
– Omar Khayyam

The sea was beautiful this day, the deepest blue you ever saw, sparkling with a thousand or more diamonds dancing above the surface. It was my favourite scene; one I would never forget. I sat at the edge, my feet straight ahead, the ice-cold Atlantic water licking my toes.

The sun beat down on me, but I was immune to the sun, my body was a rich mahogany colour, and the rays just kissed my flesh and made me feel alive and happy. I heard the joyful sound of a child playing and let my gaze wander to where a little boy was splashing in one of the pools the sea had left behind, on its endless retreat and return.

This was the life I had dreamed of, in this moment I was a rich man, no worries in the world, at peace with all that surrounded me. Everything that had gone before me or was about to come, did not matter to me, I was at one with the universe and all energy was flowing through me as if I was the conductor for everything that was around me.

I turned to look at my wife, she was lying on a brightly coloured beach towel, her thick dark hair swept up on top of her head, her eyes closed as if asleep but I knew that within five minutes she would rise and dive into the sea to cool her body. She seemed to have an inbuilt clock; she never wore a watch but she always seemed to be in tune with the workings of her body. She would rise from a deep sleep, if she had told herself to be awake at a certain time. Exactly on the hour she had to be awake, her eyes would open and she would jump from the bed, always pleased that her system never let her down.

I on the other hand relied upon alarm clocks, they were my friend and enemy rolled into one, they dragged me screaming from a world of dreams but allowed me to conduct my life as I needed to.

As if reading my mind, I saw my wife stir and rise toward the sea, her body undulated like the waves as she walked and as ever the sight of her half naked body blew me away. She was the most beautiful woman I had ever seen and age never seemed to quell this thought in me.

Although we had two children and she was nearer forty than thirty, she was still a goddess to me. My body never got used to her and the mere kiss from her lips; I was back in the first heat of passion, my mind gone and my sex taking over. A long time she had started something in my soul and of someone who knew nothing I encountered heaven.

We had met when we were young, only just out of our teenage years. I can still remember to this day what she wore, a grey pencil skirt with an emerald green silk blouse. But it wasn't her clothes that drew me to her. It was her smile, as welcoming as a warm summer day and as deep as the ocean. Her eyes were green and held countries and rivers within them, they simply lit up my world. When she spoke the warmth of her spirit blew into me like a sirocco wind. The curves and fragrance of her body captivated me and this beautiful woman with a sensuality that eclipsed the room, blew me away. Brightness poured out of her as if she was burning inside, like the sun resided under her skin.

Needless to say, within seconds I was kissing her and we never stopped talking, she became my sun and moon. I never let her go, not for one moment, for if ever she were to leave me it would be like my heart had broken loose on the wind.

Later in life, after our two children and our lives had drifted along the path we had set in motion, I knew this was the only woman I ever wanted to be with and I was the happiest man on earth.

Her Voice

"The eye you see is not an eye because you see it;
it is an eye because it sees you."
– Antonio Machado

We are now back with the man in the room and we see that things have changed. The man is now smoking, although he is not savouring tobacco but puffing furiously upon a black tube. He is frantically bringing the tube to his lips, sucking then releasing the air almost simultaneously.

His eyes dart frantically around the room, as if searching for something that might be hiding there, something he is afraid of. We also notice that he now has a television in the room. The television is off, yet his eyes when resting will look at the television in earnest, although nothing is playing for him.

The other thing we notice is that apart from sucking on the black tube, his beard has grown. We see him now in an altogether different outfit. The flowered shirt and white shorts are gone replaced by a dark bottle green sweatshirt and grey jogging bottoms. He wears a hat on his head similar to a gnome in a garden. His shoes have had their backs worn down, like someone who never opens them but just slips their feet on top of the backs.

His hair has grown, where before he was balding and short cut, now his hair is flowing towards his shoulders in wiry curls of white grey and black. His deep chocolate eyes are the same, but we cannot see life in these, they are just as the television without spark. As if waiting to be turned on with power.

Each time we have visited him so far there has been no response, we observe his actions as we would an animal in the zoo but there is no interaction. Apart from the few changes we have observed he is still a man sat in a room and we are watching him sit and wait, for what as yet we still do not know.

This time it is a different observation as we can see that things within that room have changed. As yet we do not know why or how he has changed the things we see but there is obviously something that is able to come within that room and change the things we see. Let us hope that we can solve this mystery together.

Her Voice

Memories warm you up from the inside but they can also tear you apart
– Haruki Murakami

Memories are a strange thing; they are not static entities and over time they apparently shift and migrate to different territories of the brain. Who will say that the memories I have are real or false, do I even know for sure? William Maxwell once said, "When talking about the past we lie with every breath we draw."

It is true to say that two people in love can recall exactly the same day that they met but their memories will be so different, that you would think that they had not been together at all.

I want to tell my version of events, if someone else were to tell my story, my ramblings may appear to be a false version but this is not the case. This is my truth, the ways things happened for me and this is how I recall my history, my own subjective view from the memories seared into my brain.

My truth may not be an observer's truth but it is what happened inside me and therefore is the only truth that can be told. Truth is subjective, the story happens to the person, others may see things differently but that is not the truth. That is their observation from another viewpoint. Truth can only be claimed once you see all the facts and unless you are inside a person you have no idea of their truth.

The world, in which I existed then, was quite different to the world, I exist in now. In that world I was what you would call a lucky person. Things came easily to me, be it work, money or men, I attracted everything I set my mind to and wanted. I believed strongly in the power of prayer and by using this as often as I wished, I usually found that the thing I had been praying for appeared. I never had to suffer or fight, good things just seemed to happen to me.

It was something I suppose I took for granted, if I really wanted something badly, I would put my whole heart into praying for this and even though it didn't happen automatically or immediately, eventually it would become mine. So, I never needed to worry, I wasn't quite sure what worry was.

My mother though was a great worrier; she would never cease to amaze me with her worries. I used to think, how can a person worry so much about something that has never happened, may never happen? This made no sense to me whatsoever. For example, if my father didn't come home at the time, he said he would be home, her worrying would commence within half an hour of his absence.

This would grow by notches each ten minutes, her face becoming contorted with the fruitless worry, her shifting feet making endless circles. At these times there was no consoling her by saying he is probably stuck in traffic, to her the most horrible unimaginable thing had happened and only when he walked through the door would her face dissolve to calm, when she realised that nothing disastrous had happened.

She would be like this throughout her life. If I had a sore throat it was probably throat cancer, and needed checking out by the doctor, until her worry would come under control again. It must not be easy to live like that, her sleepless nights over problems would show in her face the next day and no matter how many times she was told not to worry, she inevitably would. It was part of her make-up, the essence of her. If the worry ever turned into a real concern, then this was a relief for her, she could then concentrate all her energies into resolving the problem, worries were left far behind; she had bigger things to deal with.

No, it was the constant everyday worries that would grind her down. And I used to think, how can anyone live in such a distorted reality where nothing has happened and you are living a life of make-believe? For to expound so much energy on the fiction inside your head, I saw as a waste of all the other positive things she could put her energy into.

So, in my worry-free world it was difficult to understand the concerns of others, now I know with a deep understanding what worry is but then I was totally carefree, I had never encountered concern and therefore was naive and innocent of how this could affect a life.

When the change came it crept through the back door of my consciousness. It did not come with a trumpet and fanfare and shout to the highest tops that I am here to change your world forever. It came with subtlety and stealth, like a tarantula it started to weave its web inside my head, its gossamer threads floating through my brain's circuitry.

My earliest memory of a change was the bathroom. I was in the kitchen moving the cups from the lounge and getting ready to go to bed. Switching the lights off in the kitchen, I made my way into the bathroom for a final pee before I went to bed.

As I sat on the toilet, I noticed the tiles out of the side of my right eye, dissolving. I blinked twice then turned my head to look fully at the tiles over the bath. Sure enough the tiles were not solid; they shimmered and flickered as though there were no substance to the tiles anymore. I felt that if I stood up from the loo and reached over to the bath, I could put my hand right through the tiles and that the world I was in would dissolve. I did not do this however, I just sat and stared at the iridescent glimmer that was in front of me, I could not understand what was happening.

How could the things that I was seeing on a normal day to day basis change their structure to become fluid immaterial things? My reality was changing to another but I had no understanding of this.

I must have sat in the bathroom for at least two hours, eventually they became solid again. I rose and went to bed but this first vision lingers to this day as vivid as if I were in that bathroom now.

I think this was the first time the change made its appearance in my life. There could have been subtler events than this but to be honest as a person who lived a very normal life up to that point, I think it would have had to be something pretty strong to wake me up from my dream that everything I had seen or thought up to that point was real.

Reality now, it seems to me, is believing something is real, therefore you live your life accordingly and thought very strange if you suddenly deny everything that you can see, touch and feel around you is not real.

I mentioned this the following day to him, as you would, with something that had a profound effect on your mind. It was dismissed as so often these things are, as probably the onset of a migraine, or a fault with my vision late at night. It is very easy to accept alternative explanations and put things to the back of your mind, if you are not a worrier like my mother. She would have definitely been at the doctors the next day thinking a brain tumour. But it is very easy for each and every one of us to explain away strange happenings and never think of them anymore.

And I would have, as I had no idea at that point the change was entering into me, it is only now looking back on my life that I realised why it tried to distort my reality, it was preparing me for the change. It was giving me lessons that I needed to learn about what is reality and how once you escape a world, you enter into a new world, the same but definitely not the same.

The sickness came not long after this. This sickness was no imaginary, dissolving, out of this world sickness it was only too real. The sickness was unforgiving and cruel, an acute excruciating physical hurt, a piercing torment that went to the depths of my being and took over me. I could not stand any sound at all; sound was like a thousand cats fighting in your ear drums. The pain inside my face was so acute I couldn't even find solace in a soft pillow; it was like the pillow was made of rocks. I tried meditation, but the sickness was stronger than anything my mind could throw at it, the silken strands of the spider had taken hold and my brain was a prisoner by then. I vomited every morning, afternoon and evening as the sickness enveloped me in its grasp.

Only by facing the change would I eventually be free of it, but I did not know that then, this came much later to me. Wisdom is never so easily won and in some people it is never gained at all. I fought with all my heart against what was happening to me, but so little did I know my enemy, and that it would not allow me a fair fight.

Her Voice

A photograph, a drawing with light

Is it time to talk about the photograph? I am not sure.

The photograph was important to him and to her. It became a barrier and the cultural differences between them. The photograph represented what his family wanted for his world; it also became the metaphor for all the differences between them.

The first time I saw the photograph all my senses were enraged. It went against every single thing I had learned about love. It made me insane with jealousy and insecure about how attractive she was in the whole scheme of things. Imagine pitting someone against a photograph.

The vision still trembles in my eyes like the mirroring surface of water.

In the one corner you had a quite attractive brunette with a different culture, different way of thinking, warm, friendly, open heart. In the other corner you had a quite attractive brunette with the same culture, the same way of thinking, warm, friendly, open heart. Now let me see how easy would it be to go with whom your parents chose for you.

But there were not only photographs of this young dark-haired beauty. Oh no, there were gifts as well, music to join their souls, letters to make him realise how strong their cultural bond was.

But it was the photograph that incensed me; this was proof that his mother and father didn't want me in his life. Looking back now, would things have been different if he had never met the different girl, would the change never have troubled them? Would it have shook his head and said I will not change their world? No-body can be sure.

All his instincts told him to go against every part of his upbringing and bring the foreigner with nothing in common into his life.

He used to say, "I have gone against every part of my make up to be with you." And this was true, he had chosen the one he wanted to be with, with complete freedom, against every advice he was given, against every cultural part of him, he chose the girl, the complete opposite in mind and culture.

His instincts though always told him that this would be a great sacrifice and maybe it was, as his path in life with the opposite dark-haired beauty was not easy. It was probably more interesting though, and more loving, and had greater wealth than he ever expected.

We cannot go back to the man in the room just yet; you need to learn more things. But I have looked in and he is still there, he is not puffing furiously upon his tube at this moment in time, he is calm and contemplative, I think he is waiting for his story to be told.

So, let us read now what he wants us to hear, he climbs from the page in between the lines and writing and becomes the author.

His Voice

"Paranoia is just a heightened sense of awareness"
– John Lennon

I am being poisoned with the air in this room. I really cannot breathe, if I don't use the tube, then the air will come now and it will kill me. How can this be happening to me; we are now in the twenty-first century and yet people are allowed to kill other people by poisoning their air?

This cannot be correct. I dare not say anything to anyone about this at the moment, as I am not sure who knows about the poison in the air and who thinks that they are breathing normal air. I have so much sympathy for the people that don't know that their air is being poisoned, but who am I, to tell them?

They need to work this problem out for themselves, the way I have. The way I see it we are each and every one of us responsible for our own lives, and as I cannot trust who are my enemies and friends, then I have to make the choice, to not tell anyone of this air problem. I mean it could just go away, no disaster, nobody dies.

If people started to die around me, I suppose I should have to say at that point that there is a problem with the air. But as yet nothing, nobody is gasping for breath or complaining that the air is toxic, people are going about their everyday lives unaware of the knowledge I have.

This leads me to believe that it is only me that is being given the poisoned air, what makes me so important that they would want to kill me? I know they have already hacked my computers and the TV has been taken over, which is one of the reasons I never turn it on.

But what I don't understand is how they are poisoning the air. I think it must be through the air conditioning system but how and more importantly why, are they targeting me?

I tried to sign to her today, to tell her the danger she was in and that she should not talk. But she didn't seem to understand me. We sat for two hours with me breathing through the tube, desperately trying to get her to understand, but unable to communicate directly to her.

Finally, I flicked my thumb towards the outside, she understood the sign and we made our way out to a hill outside of my room and we sit on the grass.

The hospital gardens were the only place where smoking was allowed, strange really as every patient and staff on this hospital ward smoked. So, you can imagine the traffic through to the garden area that was littered with cigarette butts.

It also occurred to me that people believed that breathing my smoke-filled air was killing them, yet I was the one called crazy.

Finally, I told her of my fears and I asked her to find a way to get me out of this place but as usual that impassive gaze. She has no comprehension of the dangers I am facing. She looks at me so tenderly with all the compassion in the world.

Two of my friends join us and we discuss science and philosophy, my two favourite subjects. We talk about how life was created from amoebas and my friends have a great deal to say on the subject. She sits back, listens and contributes nothing to the conversation, which is lively and stimulating to say the least. All my thoughts of saving my breath have gone, now I just want to talk in the open air.

When my friends depart after smoking a cigarette, I once more tell her that I am slowly being poisoned, and cannot speak inside the place, and have to use the plastic tube. She listens once again to my fears and I even show her the ways they are doing it through the air conditioning system. But once again she nods her head and tries to pacify me with, there is nobody out there trying to poison you.

I ask her if she will help me, I know she knows what is happening to me, this is the person I trust more than anyone in the world, she sits, listens and isn't shocked. She tells me to be patient, not to worry about the air; she is sure it is safe and then she turns her back on me and walks out of the room. The last time she had spoken to the doctors for me and was allowed to take me home, but not this time why? Could it be she? Could my love really betray me, why would she want me dead?

Some people leave you with a tender touch, other people leave you with a bullet hole.

It was at this time we became ringmasters of uncertain borders, encircling our battle stations.

Her Voice

I am not me, but if I am not me, who am I pretending to be?
Does my face wear a mask, where people will ask?
I cannot think so, people only judge upon a face level.
You play the game, you are not the same, but you try to be.
I am not me, but nobody knows, I don't shout it out.
I am aware of the fact, that I put on an act, shush not a
word.
If somehow it escapes, I will not lie, I simply am not I.

After the shimmering tile episode, which was dismissed from my mind for a brief period, life carried on as usual. We led busy lives, our own business, two children, a normal family life.

Except I have since learned, in this other world that I inhabit now, that my life before was not normal. I had left the umbilical cord of my street and followed migrating birds flying in formation. I left knowing I would never return, and was astonished that the world just carried on, business as usual.

This alternate world has some things wrong with it in my eyes, so this is not normal for me either. It has a different reality to the one I am used to; it looks the same but things are different. I am not happy here, I would love to be able to go back to my world, I think I should start to make plans about how I do that.

Nobody talks, I mean really talks; in this world I am in now. Of course, many people talk, but it is so insubstantial, it's like candy floss at the fair, nothing has any meaning. Sometimes I feel like an alien that is visiting this new world, just so that I can study the behaviour of the people here. It sometimes makes me sad to listen to the normality around me, but sometimes, just occasionally, it makes me feel safe.

I go to cafes now, and listen avidly to conversations to see if anyone thinks at all like me, but after ten years in my new world, I realise few people are interested in ideas.

Matter is important, what we eat, what we see on television, the economy, our health, what one person is doing to another person, sex, drugs, and rock 'n' roll. These seem to be at the heart of the conversations I hear now, there is nothing deep about these conversations, they are real.

What we are going to eat for lunch, what was on TV last night, who has done what to whom, these are normal in this world, these are the conversations that keep things real. I try to make conversation like this, stitching myself into the mediocre, but find it difficult.

I realise I have a hole in my chest, it is so deep and far reaching that I don't feel that I have any internal organs. I am like a kid's drawing of a person with a round body but with only the outline, nothing fills the centre. Sometimes my soul moves but only to smash against the walls of this village.

I used to talk a lot, not that he would understand me normally. In fact, he would more often than not tell me to save it for another time. I used to drive him crazy with my philosophy and research into science and quantum physics.

Not that I was an egghead or anything like that, but ever since I did a Psychology course in my teens, I have been fascinated by the brain and its power. I would read and read and put my thoughts down on the ideas that popped into my head. My brain went a lot faster in the old world, my old world.

In that world, ideas would spin out of me; I could never be bored. I had a quest to find the truth in everything, how could anyone ever be bored, trying to find out the deep questions that have confused scientists and philosophers forever.

I never thought I would answer the profound intellectual questions, no never that. I just loved to research all the different viewpoints in religion, philosophy and science and then try to make my own philosophy of what I would read. A complete agnostic listening to all viewpoints, picking the ones I liked and adapting others to fit theories of my own.

But I had nobody else to talk to about these things and I found them so interesting. It was difficult to say the least to comprehend them, let alone tell somebody else about the ideas philosophers and scientists had on so many subjects.

So, he became the ears to my voice on the subjects. I would test out stuff on him and he would always argue from his strong atheist standpoint. He would always tell me that at the end of the day when we are dead, we are dead, lights out, nobody at home, and nothing, zero, zilch, for an eternity.

I could never believe this, his standpoint, for one of the things I learned was that energy cannot be created or destroyed. This is the first law of thermodynamics known as the conservation of energy law. Energy can only be transferred or changed from one form to another. So, I could never understand how my energy could leave me and not continue to exist. Rather I thought, that when I die my energy does not just dissipate, as it has no reality other than me. So, I or my energy must exist in an altered form.

Strange that I know, absolutely, as a fact now, that you can be dead and not even have died.

I'm finding it hard to hold back now and edit myself, forgive me if I start to ramble. In this weak alternative world, I am empty and lost, every day I place my heart onto the scales of conscience, waking up to each day, carrying my suitcase full of yesterday.

This alternative world seriously bores me, the days slip by like ice cubes, to a near identical picture, of *The Scream*, by expressionist artist Edvard Munsch. It doesn't have the tumultuous orange sky and to be quite honest my head isn't that misshapen, but the artist said when he painted this, he sensed an infinite scream passing through nature. From my boredom in this new universe, I too, sense my internal infinite scream passing through this new land, unheard by passers-by on the street.

I am overlooked by the talking heads inside the cafes, ignored by the bartenders and shopkeepers of this brand-new world. In this world it is easy to appear normal. You just have to know the rules. Answer a question with the appropriate response and correct manner or nod or smile when the time is right. Make appropriate sighs or groans when things seem to be negative.

Make sure you wake for the day, socialise only when necessary. Keep any talk of ideas to a minimum, for I have learnt if you persist here with new ideas, you will be thought very strange.

You may talk of family, what you eat, what was on TV, people that you know and what they are doing. Oh, and I forgot food, as that is a very important thing in this new world. Strange that, as it was what I did for a living in my old world, yet I have never felt the need to talk about the food I eat. But in this new place it can take hours to discuss, I suppose in this new world I am in, they need to remind me of home.

There is one topic in this new world that has everybody interested, it is called gossip. If you know something about an acquaintance or friend that may or not be true, and it puts the acquaintance in a negative light, it will be hurled upon like a pack of savage dogs. The truth or non-truth of the story has no matter; it is the fact that the words are out there. Like dogs fighting over the last fragment of a bone, this story will be torn apart, then put back together and chewed over to the satisfaction of the storyteller and the participants.

The one saving grace of this is that everybody seems to have a turn in being the last fragment of bone. It maybe my turn tomorrow, will I hang my head in shame, knowing that I am the subject of everyone's conversation? I'm not sure yet whether or not I have accepted the rules of this new place, so perhaps I will, perhaps I won't.

Did I tell you that they speak a different language here? I no longer speak in my native tongue, a new me talks now with words that are foreign to my old world. I find it strange that I sometimes forget my old language and have to fight to recall a word in my native tongue. I suppose this alienates me even more from my other world, I now speak and have learnt the culture he was born into. This language allows a different part of who I am to be told to others. It feels like I am talking but making it up as I go along. My words do not seem definite to me, I think I come across as a different person to who I am. For example, I have a very good grasp of my own language and use words I feel are appropriate, to what I want to say.

With this other language I have to bend the words that I know in this language, into the message that I am trying to get across. In doing this I seem to lose my original intention and I think people in this world think I am slightly naive. I am using the tools that I know to drive my point across. Yet in doing so I lose my original meaning and I have to fudge the words into ones that I know to carry the message. So, I think I come across as less intelligent and forceful than my real nature. I think I am correct, as people think I am sweet when I talk, I cannot recall any time in my own language people thought of me as sweet!

And now I am the foreigner, now I am living and teaching myself his culture and in doing so I have cut myself apart from my old self. Now even my thoughts can be split between the two languages and cultures, I am now him. I do not think the same, talk the same, eat the same, act the same.

I have basically become a new person, the old me has died. This is how you can die and yet still be alive.

The days like heavy barrels roll on by, yet here I stay following the clocks of the dandelions. But just sometimes when I am trapped inside the clock and being driven crazy by my thoughts, I remember your mouth soft and warm and how the first taste of your lips intoxicated me.

Tripping over my self-loathing, I slip sunshine into my pocket and chase the breeze on the summer wind, my heart once more alive now, knowing what pretend means.

One other thing that has me perplexed here is the lack of will to do anything. He and I worked all of our lives from the age of thirteen onwards. We never thought twice about not working it was a way of life; it gave us the money to enable us to get to where we wanted to go. Maybe the people in my new world don't take holidays because they have no need to experience anything else? Everyone says I am living in Paradise, how strange that it is not the Paradise I ever thought of.

My list of the differences could go on and on but I'm sure you will end up like *The Scream* as well, so let me say there are many differences to this world, and as I mentioned before, I need to find my way back to me. I always thought there was no way back from a black hole, once the energy has entered the event horizon, nothing can escape. But I am going to try and find a way back to my world.

I also know that this alternate world in which I live now is not my real world. How can I make my way back to where I was, can somebody tell me? I know the person I was, is now dead here, how do you make a life knowing you are dead? I feel like I am looking through distant windows like a dumb witness, memories now stapled to my tongue with secrets.

So, I hang around the old café's, sitting on cobbled streets, where the night air caresses the skin like warm silk. Meeting acquaintances and passers-by, drinking espressos or vodka, going up and down streets and discussions. Aromas of coffee and brandy perfume the air, sounds of pastries crackling and chunks of ice clinking.

A grizzled bear of a man sits in a corner playing on his harmonica a lilting tune. The men full of beers and brandies argue over football, food and fishing. The women more closed, bristle and cast knives with their eyes at the short skirts spread over the bronzed legs of the younger women.

The prostitutes here, old and young, hold their heads up high and entertain the married men. There is one prostitute here that fascinates me, she is not young but not yet too old to be unattractive. She has a lover who keeps her but she tells me she just likes sex and killed her former husband because of her desires. She is not native to this place and every year goes back to her land to get plastic surgery done.

It maybe a little unkind, if I said that she really should do some work on her face. But that is by the by, the last time she returned she had her bottom filled with implants, her bottom is now twice the size it was before she left. Now her mini-skirts incorporate this huge bottom over dimpled thighs. On an earlier visit she returned with enlarged breasts spilling out of a crop top. Every man in the café could not help but stare at this malformed forty-something-year-old showing so much flesh, that if she were at a meat auction she would have come in now at a very handsome price per pound.

Yet still the number of men that buy her drinks and listen to her stories of sexual encounters is something to see. She has one married man in particular that she always meets at the café. He is married, just there to buy her drinks, yet she holds him in the palm of her hands. A deliberate lowering of her top, or opening of her legs, he cannot take his eyes off her.

One night as the amber lights of the café begin to splutter and spark, an old lady with a lacework of wrinkles, downed her whisky sour, puckered her red lips and headed for my table. I was sitting alone with only the reflection in my glass to keep me company.

She asked if she may sit down. I offered her the chair next to me and waited to hear her story, for this lady loved to talk and storytelling was her favourite way of passing her years.

She took a hold of my hand and turned it palm upwards, then recounted a story about a young girl who made a wish for true love amongst the almond blossom trees. When the blossoms began to fall the wish was borne unto the breeze and the Universe heard the wind's call. The wish tossed and turned until the wind subdued and found a man praying on his knees filling his whole being with love. On that day he left his country and travelled far and wide, until one day he arrived at the girl's home-town. The girl was working in her father's inn and when the young man entered, the two recognised each other immediately. Scratching the glass of their dreams, they both heard the village bells ring.

At the end of her charming story, she patted my hand and said there is nothing stranger than love and where it will take you.

She told me to hold true to myself for the universe had things in store and with another pucker of her crinkled red lips she waltzed into the night.

I wish she had stayed as I wanted to tell her on this sad evening, how bright the line of fate on my palm once shone.

This life has changed me, to where I want to drink to obliterate boredom, go to bed with strangers, detach myself from people and not care what anyone else thinks. I am no longer of the age where I constantly seek other people's approval. The only real people left in my life that have the ability to rein me in, are my parents, but I left them a long time ago.

There are groups of English people who have made their homes here and enjoy the different pace of life. I can divide them into three groups. The first group are running away from something, I probably belong to this group. The second group have come to build their lives here and make a living, this group is by far the most changing, as depending on their luck they can be gone within a year or actually make it their home. The third group are either very wealthy or retired. The first and second group do try to learn the language in order to survive, the third group can be here twenty years or more and still not speak a word of the language of the country that they live in.

I find it quite hard to make friends here, acquaintances abound but for me friendships need time. I have a small group of friends that I have known since I was a young girl, I still contact. But I miss our girly chats, our night's out and the ease of their company.

Trapped in a jungle of foreign sound it is hard to connect anymore. Some days the language is like a pneumatic drill, it pierces my brain, I just want it to stop and my language to appear to calm me down.

Having set fire to the boat of my feelings, I flounder in a sea of desert sand. Sometimes I sit on the rocks by the sea, my personal rock sat on my back, heavy and cold. Distant memories wash in with the tide, curling tendrils of days long gone, enter my mind. Then they ebb into the distance as the shoreline recedes leaving me desperately trying to grasp the memories pre-rock.

Other days I just wait for the clocks hands to turn and open the vodka bottle, raising my glass to the moon, I ponder on the meaning of so what and wonder what he is doing.

Her Voice

"Vision is the art of seeing what is invisible to others."
– Jonathan Swift

I don't want to be selfish with my narrative, he deserves to speak also. Give me a little time and you will be able to know him better.

What makes a particular person go crazy? I know what the answer would be from my neighbours, without a hint of embarrassment, your dogs barking. Another person would say the sound of a tap dripping, somebody else may say the drug they just took. It takes a multitude of things to make somebody crazy. We don't have buttons in our head that say if you press this, I will go crazy, this is my crazy button, do not press or you will make me crazy. So why when my life started to crash around me, did I feel I went crazy?

The day the building moved was a huge turning point in my life. Apart from the tiles dissolving everything had continued as normal, nothing prepared me for what was about to happen. In and of itself, a building moving when not preceded by an earthquake would be a pretty big deal in anyone's life.

I mean, I'm not talking about a substantial little garden shed being picked up by a crane and moved to some other part of the garden. I'm talking of a huge black and white, timber framed Victorian property. Built over three storeys' high, in the centre of a market town, next to a bank and opposite the local market stalls.

"I saw the building move," he told me with tears in his eyes, he feared that the building we rented was not safe anymore. He had seen apparently another further up, near to the cinema, move as well, but it was only when ours started to move that his concern kicked in.

I knew that there was subsidence in the town from all the underground salt mining that had been done and there was a history in the town of the ravages that had been done by the subsidence but it still seemed to me unlikely.

He looked at me petrified, unable to stop the tears flowing, as he dreaded our building collapsing upon people and the people not being able to escape. I tried to calm him, tell him he was mistaken, that buildings don't just suddenly up and move. But he was convinced, the building had moved and we had to sell the restaurant as fast as we could and get out. He told me that he would not set foot back in the restaurant; we had to sell it there and then.

The restaurant had been our second venture; we had started out looking for another restaurant, ten years after we had sold our first. We wanted a family, and stability, and a means to be able to support me giving up work. Remember I told you about the photograph; keep this in mind as I relate the next part of his story.

He came from a large family, six brothers in all, and goodness knows how many aunts, uncles, cousins etc. Suffice to say it was a huge family, and not of my culture, I was the different one.

We decided to open another restaurant, but this time, we would ask his brothers who were also in catering to join us in this venture. We saw it as a means of making the most of the family talents as we were all in the same business and each had our own talents to bring to the business.

The only thing was that his brothers didn't have any money. I was the only one who was able to invest a substantial amount of money to enable us to open the business. We talked it over with two of the brothers and we decided that for one we would give a loan as a deposit to buy into the partnership, the other one was able to get a loan for the same amount to invest. So, they each put in ten percent of the cost of the business and he and I put in the rest. At that time, I suppose I was naive, I thought we were all family, and OK I put in the largest investment, and OK it was our house the bank loan was upon. But we were family, and if you cannot trust your family, who can you trust?

But the difference I learnt was that they were family, I was the outsider, I was the one not to be trusted.

I was not the photograph; I did not have the cultural background to accept dominance from men. I look back at the ashtray argument, such a stupid argument that nobody else would probably think twice about but for us it was a cultural difference. The fact that we were sat equidistant in reach of this ashtray, and the fact he told me to pass it to him, no words of please, made me think twice. Here I was at exactly the same distance from the ashtray as him yet he told me to pass it to him.

Now I have no qualms being asked to do anything within reason and as long as it is asked in a kind way. But I had never before been told what to do by a man and the pass me the ashtray became a huge thing for me. So, I said no, get it yourself, and for the first time I saw the difference. As I didn't just say no to him, I said no in front of his mother, father and brothers. The look on their faces was as if I had just slapped him in the face.

The other difference was that after lunch on a Sunday, in a tiny terraced house near Moss Side in Manchester, all the men would occupy the sofa and chairs. His mother and I were supposed to sit on the floor.

This was so far from anything I had experienced that shock made me sit on the floor, the first time. But on the way home we had our first argument, he told me this was his culture, I told him that this was not mine. It was never stalemate with us, he bended, understood my argument and I was never made to sit on the floor again.

So, to the night I overheard, what I wasn't supposed to hear.

The family was there to go through the final preparations for buying the restaurant; it was supposed to be a celebration as we knew at this point the bank was going to back us. I excused myself from the lounge and went to have a shower to get ready to celebrate.

As I walked into my bedroom, which was next to the lounge, I heard them discussing things but it was not a relaxed celebratory discussion. Their voices had a certain urgency, they were talking in low voices and I sensed that something was being said, that they did not want me to hear.

I pressed my ear up against the wall. They were talking in English, thank goodness, so I listened to him betray me. His brothers did not want me in the business, they told him that I would damage it and that he needed to keep me out of the business. I heard him say that he agreed with them and that I would not be a problem.

They needed my money; they needed my accountancy skills but apart from that he had to keep me to the back of the business and not have a voice. I listened to this man whom I had been with for over ten years sell me down the line to his family; it was as if I was nothing. He just wanted my money and skills and to open the business with his brothers but I was allowed no say.

There is no thought in me at this point in this other world, as to who was right, and who was wrong, it just was. That was the photograph and the cultural difference, which made us who we were.

This is why I asked, if he had continued with the same, would any of this have ever happened?

I was supposed to keep my mouth shut but I couldn't.

Maybe none of this story would have been told. But it did happen, and the Devil, God, Counting, The Trinket men, The Poisoning, The Time Machine did happen.

History or his story which one shall I choose? Are they the same, are they both not collective memories of the past lived? I would counter no, as one is objective or supposed to be, if it isn't filled with propaganda for a new age. The other is subjective, if it's not filled with covering over the nasty bits.

Do we learn from history? I would say that we do not, we still continue with wars, knowing that they increase problems, not decrease. He and I would still argue on a day-to-day basis about what was fair and just in our relationship.

Countries continually argue about what is just whilst deceiving their enemies about what they really are fighting for. A war or an argument does not determine who is right or wrong, it only determines who has won the battle at the end of the day. The victor or winner is not necessarily the person in the right, it is the person with the greater force, be it personal, military, intelligence or money.

So, history or his story, could so easily be rewritten. Your truth is never another person's truth and don't you think that is sad, that the only voice for his story should be the person left with the greater force? From him, the most intelligent man I ever met, with the greatest force and personality all of his life, left to a person, me, whom now has her voice inside an alternate world and speaks in a foreign language.

Our past so full of love and energy and life, we had no idea what an apathetic void the future would be.

Her Voice

"For she had eyes and chose me."
– William Shakespeare

I want to ask him if he remembers the wall, he replies that he does. It was so long ago and made up of huge grey cement slabs. This wall seemed to go on forever; it was the backdrop for our love. One clouded day after travelling to Wales, we stopped at a port called Fishguard in Wales. We went to a nearby beach, where he placed his hand in mine and said, "Come, let us listen to the pebbles' secrets."

It was a loving moment in a space full of truth, the mellowing sun was so gentle on the eye. We sat on the rocks and watched a soft pink sunset pass us by.

A bottle of Chablis was laid to rest on the rocks and our picnic crumbs were now food for the birds. He laid his head upon my breast and we heard faint music reaching us from a village afar. He swept me up to dance and we swayed in motion to the sound of the waves.

As the sun was bleeding red rivers into the sky and the sea like rose glass brushed the sand, we walked back to the

49

hotel. Standing against the wall, he wrapped his arms around me and pressed me against it, I could feel his passion rising. With his lips on mine I melted; gently stroking his hair from his eyes I strained to hear his soft-spoken words.

"I love you," he said, and he meant it. How beautifully you offered me the moon as I blinked away my tears of joy. We stayed a long time pressed against the wall, until the sun stamped on the sea and the stars flickered a million greetings to us.

That night under a blanket of black velvet, passion mounted from the drumbeats within. Summer and the wall lay outside our window and the sticky air clung to our skin. His beautiful eyes watched me dance with abandon to tunes on the radio.

The small fan we had hummed like an agitated insect, and we sat naked eating peaches and oranges, the juice trickling like a river down our bodies. We graced our sex with cigarettes and songs, our feelings whirling like waltzers at the fair, whilst birds took flight from the fields of our souls.

After we made love, I quivered like an aspen tree and after 7670 nights I finally shared a bed with the meaning of love. Overlooking the wall, day and night, night and day, we were inseparable, everything I was, he complemented and everything he was, I complemented.

One night as we were lying in bed after making love, I was tickling the hair on his chest. Reaching over to the bedside cabinet I lit each of us a cigarette. As he thanked me, the music of breathing disappeared, and I felt this huge burst of emotion, a flag was suddenly waving in my heart. On the verge of tears, I had to tell him that I loved him, I loved him with all my heart and soul. He had rocked my world until I capsized, filling my world with endless colours, magic now held me under his wing.

There was a photograph in this alternative world that had pride of place in my house here. But unknowing people have taken this down, and put it in the bin, deeming it to be an eyesore. This was our place, the place he and I declared our love. Although the image was generic, just a displaced image, it helped me remember paradise is hard to find.

The image was of the wall and the sea, where we made love, and pledged our love. This was the romantic place on earth for me, it still is, and I was enveloped by the most handsome man on earth. He gave me everything that day I could have wished for, we were as one. He was the most beautiful man I had ever met and I was his dark-haired beauty.

Any thoughts, at that time of the other photograph, were forgotten, it had been replaced. I knew at that moment he wanted me more than anything on this earth.

If ever I could drop anchor on this sea of time, this was the moment, for I cried and died and laughed and smiled, I would live forever in the memory of those days.

These were the days of rainbows and waterfalls.

How on earth could he go back to the photograph and music at that point in time? He had either sold his soul, or he was following his path, I am not sure anymore. But what happened to us over time, was no dream, it was reality.

I try to grasp hold of this memory now to remember every detail but it is like trying to grasp sand between your fingers, it folds back into the golden blanket without identity.

Let us go back to the building moving. I gave in; I could see the panic it was causing him. I knew the stress of the restaurant had become too much over the years. I ended up the victor in the family war against me; he lost them all for years.

His mother, father and brothers nobody spoke to him, he lost his background, family and culture, not on the night I heard him betray me but within one year of the restaurant opening all was lost to him.

He never saw what he said against me as betrayal, he saw it as the best thing to do to keep the business running happily, as his family business. But with so much at stake from where I stood, I could not afford to lose a grip on the business; I needed to guide it financially.

I turned out to be right eventually, although this was not a happy day for me, as it brought huge stress and the counting. I found out two of his brothers were stealing from us. They did not leave easily, each fought against us and the whole of his family turned their heads and punished us. I believe if I hadn't been a part of the restaurant, all would have been glossed over and forgiven.

But for me I stood to lose everything, mine and my children's house and future. I could not let this happen, I had to fight and he backed me, he understood his family's betrayal and fought against the injustice of what they had done.

This was why when the building moved, it became a symbol of all the destruction the building had wrought on our lives. He saw it as a sign, the building was about to come down around our heads, and we should move on and leave the building behind, leave the past, the agonies, the separation from families behind, and start anew.

That night the building moved, he poured out all his agonies in one long night of pain. His tears and heart wrenching sobs wouldn't stop.

I could smell the whisky on his breath but knew this wasn't a part of the panic and stress that was unfolding before me because I felt scared for the first time. My stomach responded to this fear and began to roll, small fluttery movements, dancing on the inside of my flesh.

Aroused by an impending danger that I could not describe to myself, I knew something was happening and it was going to have huge implications on my life. It is easy to say that now, as I now know the future, but then without any understanding of what lay ahead, I knew the fear was only too real.

I called the emergency doctor around 5.30 a.m. and we went to see him as his surgery opened. He listened to us and prescribed medication for depression.

We went home and he was calmer but still absolutely terrified at his experience of seeing a building move.

Her Voice

"No matter how fast light travels, it finds the darkness has always got there first, and is waiting for it."
– Terry Pratchett

After the problems with the family, and the huge stress it put us under, not knowing how we would resolve things if it went to court. I started counting. I had always worked with figures and was used to calculating prices in my head when I worked behind various bars. Counting was actually always a part of my adult working life, so why would I worry when I started to count.

The thing that I have to get across was no ordinary counting. This was a huge spreadsheet counting with lists upon lists of imaginary numbers on. I would go through each of the columns of imaginary numbers in my head and add the column to the total at the end. Once that was finished, I would start on my next column and then my next column.

This of course took a lot of my attention, as I needed to be precise and needed definitely to get to the right total at the end.

My brain would fly over these imaginary columns, totalling each and every one at lightning speed in my head.

I never really realised that I could never go wrong. But looking back, how could I check for certainty if the column was correctly added up, because I was making the numbers up as I went along. So, it was almost impossible to create the same column twice, to check I was correct, although, this didn't appear to be an issue with me.

The main factor which was important to me was the counting and recounting columns of numbers in my head. But that in itself was distressing for me, as I couldn't turn my brain off and stop counting. It came to a point where I craved for peace from counting, just to be able to turn off the light and my thoughts to go to sleep.

But it never happened; as soon as I woke the counting would start, over and over and over. Not only was the counting affecting me terribly but I started to feel sound.

For example, if a door was shut outside, I would feel this in my stomach; I would hear and then feel the sound in my stomach almost simultaneously. If everything around me was noisy, I would not get the feeling but if all was quiet and a light switch was turned on, this sound in turn would appear inside of me. It was not a nice sensation; it was like a thud inside my stomach which would scare me.

My body had suddenly become highly attuned to sound waves, my skin quivered at a rustling noise, my stomach thudded at the sound of a door, my heart thumped at the sound of the doorbell, my forehead pounded at the sound of keys in a lock. My body seemed to be constructed to measure small degrees of changes in sound; an acute sensation would enter me when I heard a sound. I was living in a terrified state of counting and sensation.

The sickness was at its most malevolent at this time also, it crucified my face and jaw, nothing could pacify the pain. It continued each day, as a yearlong migraine, I couldn't bear anything harsh, be it noise, pillows, children's conversation, laughter, music, all was too much. If I had peace without sound, my head would continue its counting regardless; if I were finally asleep in the silence, my body would feel a sound and wake me up.

It was then that I found Buddhism and meditation.

This is not going to be a hard sell on Buddhism or meditation, far from it, I could never do it. Oh, but I tried, I read the first book which told me to try to listen to three sounds at once. I lay in my armchair, eyes closed, listening to a bird singing in the trees outside my window. I then tried to introduce another sound like the logs crackling on the fire, but as soon as I tried to hear the second sound, the bird sound would go, and I would be concentrating on the logs crackling, so then I would have to consciously switch to listen again to the bird singing.

I gave up after a long time of practicing hearing only two, goodness knows how people can manage to listen to three sounds at once. For me it was impossible, maybe my head and my body just can't deal with sounds.

Next, I tried breathing, I tried my hardest, I really did, to concentrate on the inhale and exhale of breath. But my mind with all of the complicated additions that were yet to be totalled, drew me away each time I attempted.

I could no more concentrate on my breathing than fly over the ocean and shoot the breeze on a sun-drenched beach with a Bacardi and coke in my hand! But oh, at that time of my life every sinew and synapse of me prayed with each breath in and out, that I could do just that.

This was the nadir of my life, there were many more after, but this seemed to herald the troubles. I tried lifting the present to the past, simply exhausted by my glass now empty in front of me. I tried to find the child with light in her eyes, thundering down the tunnel of my lifetime, calling to my childhood streets, but there was only silence.

The woman who never worried about anything reduced to a shadow world inside her head of counting numbers. Like the quote at the top of this chapter, my darkness had reached every part of my mind and body, the speed of light, no matter, that it's the fastest thing in the universe, simply could not reach my blackness.

My darkness was there just waiting for the light to be turned on but the light just wouldn't come. My body was reacting physically through sickness and sensitivity to everything, and my mind was in overdrive, neither would give me peace. I needed lightness, not this all-pervading, encompassing shadow of black, where no joy could reach me.

The change had definitely entered my life at this point; we were both being affected in our different ways. He had my hopelessness to contend with and I had my demons. Being that we were not at this point in competition to see whose situation the worse, we could not understand at all what was happening to us.

We were each alone in our own internal hell, whilst sharing every other aspect of our lives. I started to disintegrate before his eyes, but believe me when I tell you our love never wavered.

We would still talk all night, make love, lie in each other's arms, I believe that helped somewhat to keep our demons at bay, I functioned automatically to quell the worst that the change was doing, I masked a lot from him.

But make no mistake I knew it was there, it had toyed with me, it had entered me. It was only a matter of time before it would get worse.

I came from darkness, I will die into darkness, why am I living inside darkness?

One day it got so bad, the darkness now penetrated my core, intense palpable, anonymous, wrenching my insides until bleeding within. It held me within its jaws, like Cerberus it guarded my gates of hell, not letting any light enter. It's three heads, fear, sorrow and pain glaring at me knowing I am so weak. But what is a life when lived in fear, it is an abyss into which we fall praying for deliverance.

I told him that I needed to see a doctor. Now as long as I have known him, he has been against medication, he has always believed that it is better to not take, than to take. So, when I went to the doctor and he prescribed me medication, I told my doctor that my husband strongly disagreed with tablets. My doctor asked me if I could ask my husband to come back with me so that he could explain what was happening.

When we returned, my doctor explained that people from his country rarely get this illness and that it was something that I needed for now. It was only for six months but after this he would have his wife back. My husband then concurred and I began a six-month course of medication, after this I never counted again.

This was before the building moved; this was how the family stealing and punishing us, affected me. He may have coped better with his family break up than I did, but the problem I had was, I felt guilty. If I hadn't insisted on being a part, would they still have stolen from him? If I hadn't given them opportunity, they would never have had the opportunity to hurt us.

I believe that each of us our responsible for our own paths, you make up your own mind what you will take, once you have reached a threshold, you will kick back. Your decisions will affect your life; make mistakes but come away knowing they are your mistakes and no one else's.

My mistake was not to enter the business against all his family's negativity, my mistake was to think I was part of the family and try to help them. That was what I found so hard to deal with after the nuclear explosions within the family, the fall out was like death to us. We could not accept or forgive any of them for what they had done. A long time later we did, it took many years and a death but we did eventually reconcile.

His Voice

*"When the strong are too weak to hurt
the weak, the weak had to be strong enough to leave."*
– Milan Kundera

Remember I told you I could not believe she would betray me?

My thoughts upon this fact are gaining ground. She wants me to stay here!

Here in this stinking place, where nobody knows they are being poisoned, where people cry to the Gods, or ramble on about things that are not important. Where vacant eyes stare into space, language is set down in the unreal chaotic, grasping zero, other minds just floating in a mindless wave. You can see shivering universes inside their eyes, they have run for the stars on space time roads. Their howls run through the corridors, all boundaries dissolving into thin air. At night you can hear them roaring, like night winds crying, minds riding ghost carousels in the air. Medication dispensed like candy to stop them from dreaming, shuffling little steps slowing down reality.

In my first moments of being lost here, it felt like I was flying, a year in my mind was gone in a day. Ideas colliding, buzzing around like flies. My mind was a helter-skelter where the light became sunrise and all was too bright to be contained there. My nerves jangling with too many wires, I only watch now from the corners of my eyes.

The food is inedible, because of the poison, and the TV is on all day and night. I used to love television, but here it is not like entertainment, nobody really watches it. Well, that is not really true, as in our pyjamas on high backed chairs we would all stare at it. What we did not do is interact with it, we may just as well have been staring at the creatively painted blank white walls.

Occasionally a patient would come in with a relative, sit down and talk quietly. You could soon spot the outsider as they would comment, for conversation, about what was happening on the screen. The rest in the room would just continue staring as though nothing had been said.

The white walls here are infused with a faint lemony bleach odour, locked cabinets, sealed doors and barred windows. I have my own bedroom here but that does not make me feel less secure. It may be that only my air conditioning system is being poisoned.

After some time and medication, I got a day pass, this allows you to leave the facility for a few hours. At these times I would go and buy alcohol and sit on a park bench in the middle of the town. In those hours I would meet enemies disguised as friends, watch the buds sprout on the blossom trees and jump in front of cars to make the drivers wake up.

Occasionally supervised by my wife and daughters, I got a night pass to go out with them. One night we went to a Chinese restaurant in the town near to the hospital. I think the night started OK, but I did not feel comfortable, I was anxious.

The more the evening passed the more my anxiety levels rose. It felt like the chef in the kitchen was going to poison me, a Trinket man was whispering in my ear. As the food came to the table the Trinket man became more insistent that I should not eat the food. I told my wife and daughter not to eat the food and asked if I could speak to the chef.

I could tell my wife and daughters were becoming uncomfortable as we had owned a restaurant, we made it a rule never to complain to others unless absolutely necessary. But the thoughts were coming too strong, the Trinket man was insistent that the food should not be eaten. When the chef came to the table, I accused him of trying to poison us.

My family apologised and we left the restaurant. Grateful for my victory, I allowed myself a smile inside that I was able to protect them.

But let me ask you, how often have you had a little voice inside your head telling you don't do this, or do that?

We all have our inner voices that tell us to go one way or other. The fact I give mine a name, is just the same as you saying about the angel or devil that sits on your shoulder, telling you to be naughty and eat the cream cake or telling you to be good and not eat the cream cake. We all have our inner dialogues and speech, don't we?

What I could not understand was why my inner dialogue was now so disturbing to my family.

I have a meeting tonight with her and our daughters; they are coming in to see me. What do I do? Do I tell her what I know?

I want to trust her; I want to introduce her to a friend I have made here but I also want her to take me home with her. What do I say to get her to take me home with her, how can I get her to know how I feel? She didn't seem bothered the last time, when I told her I was being poisoned, I need her to help me go home, all I want is to go home.

She absolutely knows how important that is to me. I have told her on many occasions, and given her all of my notes, these explain all. These notes are made up of diagrams the Trinket men passed to me, as he would talk, I would talk about other realities I would draw pictures of what he spoke. What I really want is it to be the two of us, and for us to talk, really talk and her to understand.

Once the button is pressed and the nurse lets my life into this place, I look at the three of them. My whole life in front of me, I want to reach out and hug but something stops me. I am wary; I believe one is a betrayer.

I lead them into a room that is not being used; they sit and look at me as if awaiting some sort of reaction. I ask them to take me home. I watch intently for a reaction from the betrayer. She says nothing.

My daughters ask how I am, I respond quickly, immediately, I want to go home, I don't want to be here any longer. I must get home, but my girls look from left to right, never in the eye and then look to the betrayer to see what she thinks. I realise there and then she has got to them, she has turned their heads, my girls believe the deceiver.

What should I do now? The stakes are high; each part of my life is now against me in that room. I want to scream at them, force my personality onto them, so they know that I am still the man they have always known.

At that point my friend walks through the door to say hello. I welcome the respite and company so we can collect our thoughts.

My friend says hello, and tells the girls how beautiful they are, this is true and I feel so proud of them as she says this. She tells them that she makes perfume and that she will go and get each of them some perfume from her room to give to them. My daughters notice her bear.

My friend looks at the bear and says, "Yes this is my baby girl, I am so proud of her, do you not think she is beautiful?" Then she gently rocks her baby girl to her chest. After some time of showing her baby to them, she leaves the room to go and get the perfume.

My youngest daughter asks me why the lady carries a teddy bear that she calls a baby. I answer truthfully that I have no idea why a grown woman carries a teddy bear everywhere she goes but that the teddy bear must give the lady comfort.

When my friend returns with the perfume, I realise that my daughters are ill at ease with my friend, I have no idea why this should be, my friend has just brought them gifts of perfume and my daughters were not brought up to be rude to people.

My youngest daughter, I can tell is particularly nervous, I ask her why she cannot look me in the eye. She mentions that today she saw what I did and she is scared that I will repeat the earlier episode. Now I know that they are all in it together to keep me here. I ask her straight out what was so bad that I did? Once more she cannot look me in the eye, I think she is ashamed of her emotions, why is it so hard to tell someone the truth? She mumbles something about me on the floor begging for drugs or I would go crazy.

Absolute bullshit, I wanted something to calm my thoughts, on my knees begging for drugs, does she think I am an addict?

My wife now interjects and says that they need to leave. I TELL HER THAT YOU CANNOT LEAVE ME HERE. I NEED TO LEAVE AND I NEED TO LEAVE NOW.

She responds by telling my daughters to put back on their coats as it is cold outside. How, fucking cold, does she think it is in this room right now? I will not allow this, I will not allow this to happen, the traitor is going to walk out that door taking my life with her and I don't have a say?

As they dress for the cold outside, we all see my friend, with her baby, greet her husband. I think we must have all noticed the wariness of his face, similar, if not the same, to what I see in this room. How on earth can I tell them that it is not me they should be frightened of.

There are outside forces beyond our control that have now gained power and are manipulating our every move.

And so, my lives try to leave without me, their breath burns into me as they pass me. So, I hold my breath trying not to let go, for I cannot allow this to happen. As they make their way to the button, I charge after them. They cannot leave me here in this place, with these assassins, how can I get them to realise that I am going to die, if they leave me here.

I follow them up the corridor noticing the desperation in their faces as they look back towards me and open the door. I try to sprint the last five yards to reach them as the button is pressed, then I am struck from behind. As four of the enemy guards, jump on top of me and grapple me to the ground. I cannot look from this position as my life leaves the building, I just want them to help and understand me. All I could see of them were their faces shimmering through the glass.

Floating, imagine nothing, then just float. There was nothing more after that, but once I regained consciousness, I realised I had been consigned to the padded cell. My own personal safety room. *How lucky am I*, I thought, *if they manage to get to the air in here, I am doomed.*

There was only a clock visible in the cushioned room and on a quick calculation I found I had spent eight hours in the room. I had sense enough to realise that if I showed any anger or emotion this could go on a while. So as gently as I could I pushed the intercom button and asked to use the bathroom.

I need to get the girls on my side. I need them to see what is real, I need to tell them everything and I need to tell them that I am not crazy in all of this. Everything they see is real, it may be nothing they are used to, but the fact is that everything I am going through is completely real, and I need them to be on my side and help me. But how can I get them to realise that their mother is now the enemy?

I decide to obey the rules, listen to my enemies, be intelligent, do exactly as they say and then once free, take my girls as far away from here as I can. Rebuild my life with them and if it has to be leave her alone.

So, I say nothing now I am silent, I feel I have no one left to talk to, my history has something to say but the characters now are silent, like a stone I am silent, I dare not speak my truth for I offend sensitive ears, so behind walls and doors I sit in silence, chained to the day. A separation of a once unbreakable bond, I search for something but there is only silence.

Her Voice

*"I want to leave, to go somewhere where I should be really
in my place, where I would fit in . . . but my place is
nowhere; I am unwanted."*

– Jean-Paul Sartre

We are back in the room now; he is still dressed as a gnome.
Grey jogging pants, red sweatshirt, green hat, and a long
bushy beard. There is no reaction from him today. He just
sits, sits and waits. Time does not seem to have any effect on
him, it looks like he could sit and wait forever, maybe for
the next minute to arrive or just sitting in silence awaiting
something.

He never thinks backwards or forwards, the things I have
mentioned are not in his mind.

The days like heavy barrels roll on by, sorrow like a
bird, lies listless in my chest. Why is this other world so
unreal and superficial? It is as if I am living in an imaginary
world and I have lost myself and how I would act normally.

I have no sense of who I am in this world. I could say
things with certainty in the other world, that for instance I

would never have done such and such a thing but here I am not sure. I have rewritten who I am, or have I just reinvented myself? If I am now just a construct of my imagination why do I not like the person I have become here? Why did I not make myself into a happy go lucky fun person?

In my house, the shutters like eyelids are lowered over the windows. The wind catches the rain and throws it against the glass, and on days like these when there is nothing inside me, I hear in the wind a lapsed forgotten voice and feel as if I have lost my way.

I live in a beautiful place with a view of the sea, which for some people would be paradise. I wake up nearly every day to sunshine, blue summer days that pass by in a haze.

Why does the other grey world dog my every step? Why does my old self call to me, why can I just not leave this world and cross a bridge back to my old world?

Am I delusional? Is it this world or the other that is the dream world?

I remember when he started departing, his invented face strained into a smile. He buried himself inside, with one finger unconsciously drumming against his chest. His secrets built a barricade behind his eyes, his feet suddenly stilled and he stopped dancing.

He was never what you would call a great dancer, no Fred Astaire was he. But oh, how much, in the restaurant, did he love to dance. His charisma and huge personality made everyone fall in love with him. So, on fiesta nights in the restaurant, he would get everyone up to dance. His character exuded such a zest for life, his feet not resting until we went home. He would always party until the sun rose upon tomorrow and everyone else had gone to bed.

He had such a gift of making everyone just want to party and have fun, he was the greatest front man in a restaurant I had ever seen.

The night I woke up in another reality, I remember distinctly. It was quite a few years after the building moved. Even though the building moving was the start, on its own, it would have just been a memory but with all that happened afterwards it became the beginning of my journey to this other world. I have lost here, everything, which is normal and natural for me.

I also lost in that other land everything that was normal. Is this a land of fiction, can I write my life as I am writing these pages? But if that were so why am I making this life as hard as the last one was? Why am I repeating mistakes, why am I always so scared here, and what is it that I am so scared of?

It was just after the fire, a night of living hell, the door into him was still ajar on its hinges but it was as if the wind kept slamming it open and shut. A mist was rising around him as grey as a featherless bird and he was becoming invisible, making his specialist subject a silent death. His secrets had built a barricade behind his eyes and his fingers unconsciously drummed against his chest pointing their mournful beats towards his heart.

He is lost in the now, blind to the future, handicapped by that which has gone before.

Her Voice

*"A nightmare that would end is a nightmare
that would begin."*
– Al-Saddiq Al-Raddi

So, to the night I ended up in an alternate universe. It was not a night I had experienced before; he was wrapped like a mummy in bandages from the fire.

I haven't yet spoken about the fire but it was Bonfire Night and he was at work. Aimed with the task of lighting the bonfire for the hotel, he used petrol to light the fire. Hence to say the fire exploded and he was badly burnt. When he was let out of hospital his skin was like a leopard and still bleeding from the wounds he had suffered.

He needed painkillers but chose whisky instead, whilst I drunk Bacardi. I knew at that time, that we were in the grip of the change and that it would never let us go.

He was as unaware as ever that something was wrong, he could not see how the change had entangled us in its web and escape was now impossible. I had noticed small changes in him at that time, he had taken a liking to porn and had started to smoke weed. I arose one morning to find my computer now had a naked woman dancing across the screen. My hard drive kept crashing with the number of viruses the porn had infected it with. My brain kept crashing with the amount of shit; I had to put up with.

There was no time for sleep, each night for him was party night, someone would be invited over and even if I were asleep, I would get woken by one of his guests. They would inevitably climb into my bed and start to cuddle me, persisting in their stupors, that they wanted me.

They were always high on drink or drugs. I used to feel frightened and wonder why he never protected me from them but he was always as high as they were. If I told him what had happened, he would ignore me, he could not see the affect his behaviour was having on me.

He eventually gave away the restaurant away to one of these drinking pals. The morning the deal had been struck; they were both so drunk I could not get them to wake up. I remember taking them to work, knowing that they couldn't even walk, let alone cook and serve in a restaurant. But the deal had been struck, we were to give away what we had worked for ten years for.

Another betrayal but his fear from the building moving, his stress and the change were taking over his mind and life. I thought that if we were to be free of the restaurant our lives would go back to normal and we would continue our lives once more. This was never to be.

In the small hours of the morning just after he had been released from the burn unit, we were fizzing with the whole night in our veins. We had a deep conversation about all the bad things that had seemed to envelop our life. I stripped my heart naked about how things were, how the man I loved had changed so much. I threatened that night to leave him, he responded with a kitchen knife to his bandaged arms and hands.

He was deeply scarred from the burns from the fire, so I spoke softly in the darkness.

But the voices between us did not connect, they sucked the light from eyes now dead.

He sat there holding the knife to his wrists, I could not bear this. I wanted to scream and scream at him, how he was treating me, how I had lost him, how he was not my husband anymore. He sat there, threatening me with a knife held to him, I was so tired, the dramas never seemed to stop, my life was a soap opera lurching from disaster to disaster.

It was like living in an American action film, where the plot had to be continually exciting, never letting go of its grip on the audience.

Adrenalin fuelled days and nights, I will forever remember, I had lived more in four years than others do in lifetimes. My counting had long since vanished, I was awake knowing that this change until it was confronted, would continue to wreck our relationship.

He still had no idea of the effect; he was living a high every day and night on drink and drugs and porn. I was in a state of fear and tiredness.

He could not sleep, so I was not allowed to sleep, his mind would demand attention all through the night, he needed to expound his thoughts because his mind was in Formula One mode, racing so fast that I could never catch up.

The night in question, twilight began to paint the sky dark blue on blue, and our cigarette smoke whirled like wraiths to the ceiling, it was then we began to talk.

His gaze cut through me like a buzz saw, my nerves were jangling from being so wired. I saw the shadows fly from the windows; bubbles of silence arose as we let the conversation unfold.

I started looking for the drink me bottle as a glass wall began appearing between us. I looked at his face and saw eyes that had never slept, we talked, and talked. The room exhausted now by our empty glasses; the knife lay on the sofa between us.

As the moon went to bed and the horizon gave birth to the sun, I saw that I had finished a bottle of Bacardi. His empty whisky bottle lay at the side of the sofa. Our words were left hanging in the air like dust motes in the beams that the sun threw through the window panes.

I told him I was going to bed. I told him that I could no longer love him as he was. The knife still lay on the sofa between us, unused. All the bluster and fight had gone, I had made my decision, I could no longer be with him as he was.

He wasn't willing to fight the change, he had no conception of it entering him. The tablets the hospital had given were unused, kept now in so many drawers my house was as good as a pharmacy.

I remember entering my bedroom and undressing as usual, slowly heading for the clouds of my eyes. As I lay my head upon my pillow, within moments I was asleep.

Upon waking the following morning, I felt a fear that I had never before felt in my life, it shook me from my head to my feet.

The fear started as soon as I opened my eyes, I was in my bedroom but this was not my bedroom. Well to make things clearer for you, it was my bedroom but not the bedroom that I went to sleep in. Everything was the same except for the bed, the bed was the wrong way around in the room. I went to sleep with my bed against one wall and woke up with my bed on the adjacent wall.

Now this was virtually impossible as there was only one wall in my bedroom that the bed could have been against. The other two walls had wardrobes and the third wall had a long mirror and dressing table. But my bed was now on the right of the bedroom instead of being in the centre. I was pole-axed. As I awoke, I tried to calm myself about the bed, my husband had still not come to bed, I was on my own and could not account for anything that could have moved my position whilst I was sleeping.

But that was not all, I knew for a fact that my bed was still in the centre of the room, yet I knew for a fact that now my bed had turned toward the adjacent wall. I was afraid to turn around now in case I disappeared, and nothingness sat waiting behind each door, my heart beat a military tattoo. Everything was uncertain, today, tomorrow or the next moment do they exist?

How could I account for these two absolutes, how could one reconcile with the other?

All I could think of was quantum mechanics and wave particle duality. That I was seeing the particles which I recognised as my bedroom, this had mass, this was order, and ordinary, for every day of my life for over twenty years. The other I was seeing was waves, this was transferring the energy of the room into something that I had never seen before, it was making my room a replica of my room, but not as I would expect as the observer, it had somehow changed what I would have expected when I woke up.

I arose and went into the bathroom, the fear making me vomit. I then went into the lounge to see him awake, the bottle of whisky still lying in front of him, the knife still lay on the couch. I walked towards him and held him in my arms, there were no words left at that point.

The girls stirred in their beds, I made breakfast, took them for their school bus and returned to this house where I had lived so many years but which had now become a living hell.

When I walked back into my bedroom, I found that the furniture had been arranged exactly as it always was, but I knew that this was not the reality, I had known before.

The bed turning was the thing that mattered the most, even though I could see no evidence anymore of this, I knew it had been real. I was no longer in the world I had been up to this point; my world had been split off from his and I had now ended up in an alternate universe.

If we follow what he did next, this will take us on a journey with his two girls and a realisation in me that the thing wouldn't leave him alone. Then more than ever he needed my help and to disallow him his adventure, but then more than ever I needed peace, I had journeyed to another universe and could not go back to the torture that my life was.

So, one day in spring I said goodbye to him and my daughters, at the time nobody could understand why on earth I would let my daughters go with him. But you have to understand, I was trying to do the best for him and them, but also me, I needed to stop my sickness.

He always said that I had changed his culture, maybe going back to his culture would help him in the long run, my eldest child was not happy and being bullied at school, maybe that would help her, I did not want my two girls apart, maybe that would give them something for the rest of their lives. I really didn't know anymore; I just knew that I wanted them altogether.

So be it, I made the decision they could all go away from me.

And go away they did, on a journey that I believe benefited no one. My children lived a free life and my husband entered the change in its entirety. There was no place he could feel safe, this was his matrix world.

Neo, alias me, I thought it wasn't real.
Morpheus, alias him, your mind makes it real.

His Voice

"There are five billion people living on this planet. But you fall in love with one particular person and you won't swap them for any other."
– Jostein Gaarder

She has betrayed me; she won't help me anymore. They want to pump me full of drugs, poison me and make me a zombie. I knew I had to be free, but she was willing now to side with my enemies, the ones that wanted to drug me.

The first time this happened, I remember, she rescued me. She managed to talk to them all, so I would not stay in that place. She was on my side, she made them let her take me home.

I promised her if she took me home, I would be no trouble, I would take the tablets and get well.

After seeing the building move and telling her of my concerns, the doctor sent me to the hospital. I spoke to a doctor who said I could go home if I would take the tablets he would prescribe. She said that I would and we left the hospital together.

I took the tablets and within a few days I was flying. My usual self had been replaced with someone who was now running across the fields as though on air. Every second making time speed forward and I was as big as the world. I was euphoric, the storms had passed and I wanted to embrace the world. My ideas were racing around corners like Formula One cars and I wanted to become an advocate of the law.

I am not sure why but my dark-haired beauty felt a great concern for me at this time. So, I was taken back to the doctor's, this was the first time I was sent to the hospital to be assessed.

Having told a doctor about how I felt was really great, he went into my history and prescribed me some tablets. Apparently, the anti-depressants the other doctor had prescribed made me too high and they needed to bring me down.

She was always there telling everyone, how I was not acting normally. She would cry, they would pity her and there I was back on more tablets which I hated. I was insisting that I was fine there was no need for anything, but no, they took her side. I was only allowed to leave the hospital if I promised to take the tablets, suffice to say I did.

Yet on my first meeting with the Trinket men, I knew that it was not going to be my last, and that the euphoria I had felt was going to return, for who that has seen paradise would want to go back to Earth.

After the tablets had 'supposedly' brought me back to normal, I felt the need for secrets, for things were changing inside me. So, I made her my accomplice to the thoughts that I had but made her promise not to tell another soul. This was now between the two of us, as I could now see and hear things other people could not.

I felt all powerful at this time, I could do anything. I had no need for sleep, I could run for miles, I was an all-powerful human being with an inside view now on the mysteries of life. I needed now to talk to her about my new found ideas and how I thought that I was a healer and going to do God's work. I told her that I could now cope with the building moving, as I was as clever as the next solicitor and would beat anyone that said I was culpable for this.

Life became a game, I needed to know now, what she knew of all the philosophies and science that she had learnt. I begged her to teach me every night, anything that she had learnt. I brought books from the library on anything from Buddhism and hinduism to Charles Darwin Theory of Evolution.

I needed knowledge more than I ever had in my life. I also knew that God had touched me. I was no longer an atheist believing that death was the end. I was now a healer; Jesus Christ had entered me and I was on earth to do his work. The tablets never worked for me, they would not allow me to be whom I was supposed to be, so I stopped taking them. In fact unless I was forced I never took them again.

I became an authority on everything, and even the television would talk to me especially, and I would pick up all the subliminal messages the Trinket Men were trying to tell me.

She was then my saviour at this point, she kept the secrets and allowed me to expand what the voices were telling me to do. To stop all the interference in my far superior brain, I needed alcohol or weed just to calm me down or I would not be able to sleep.

But the new feelings I had at this time were the most fantastic feelings of my life. I was all powerful, I was going to sort out the world's problems, I had insight to every conspiracy in America and felt I could cure people that needed my help. God and Jesus became very important to me, I knew that God had put me on this earth for a purpose, and I knew that I embodied Jesus, he was with me all the time, I felt that now at last I could cure people.

This was probably one of the best times of my life, if this was something wrong with my brain, I could not see it. I had the best brain in the universe, I would sort out and understand all of the problems on this earth, life became so good! The possibilities spread like cancer, the more I thought about them, the more they multiplied, and there was no way to stop the thoughts, I was no longer the one in control.

So why did she think I needed help at this time?

This was a time to rejoice, understand what I was put on earth for, let her explain to me all her ideas, and then let me use them for good. Because before this, I could not even bring myself to read one page she had written. Just leave me in front of the television with an action film and that was my life.

Now I had the whole universe beckoning to me and everything she wanted me to be, so she could talk, and still, she wasn't satisfied.

In front of this landscape where all moves in me, I can feel the birth of my passionate flesh. I was stepping into life, wanting to spread my existence as far as possible.

For I am no longer who I thought I was, I am so much more. In this eternity I stand nowhere and everywhere.

After a few years of what I was thinking drumming against my flesh, was when I saw the change in her.

A thought like the breeze began to sigh, slowly, so slowly and with tender footsteps, the thoughts began to gather pace, and reverberate more and more.

This was the time that she started to watch me from the computer, there was always a blue light flashing at one of the neighbour's houses. I started to realise that this blue light was a signal that she was watching me.

There was a disturbance to my perception, as when a fox knows it is being hunted.

I could not see her watching me, I could not hear her, I just knew it instinctively, she was trying to catch me out!

But I had strengths on my side, for example, the people on the jury of a musical TV programme would tell me what she was doing. I started to see her betrayal in a very subtle manner and I knew that she was going to try and steal my liberty again.

When the mental health team eventually arrived, it came as no surprise, I knew she had phoned them. There was no way in a million years I would give them what they wanted.

They asked me about my thoughts, my smells, whether or not I could hear anything.

Are they all stupid? As if I would give at this point my inner life to them. I knew they were trying to trick me, there was nothing I would say, so I sat mute. The only person that would talk was my betrayer.

She tried to tell them what I had done or said, but for them they could not see, they were completely blind like everyone else to how far I had come, just like everyone around us, as if they would believe her!

And I was right nobody believed her, they all sat around, had tea and did not know what the fuss was about. She tried to tell them that I was the best magician in the world and I hid everything, but when they saw me calm, no problems, they just took their leave.

But yes, I was a magician, I knew that if they were to access my inner thoughts, I would end up back on the tablets. This was the last thing in the world I wanted, who wants to deaden a mind full of ideas and hope for the future with a true vision of reality?

So, I took the freedom she gave to me at this time, and used it to search for knowledge, I became very wise and cunning because I knew my life had changed to a new set of rules. I knew that I had to keep within limits with her, but at the same time I knew that my life was now changed forever and God and Jesus were within making me a better person.

There is no way ever they were going to deaden my mind again. I will keep my secrets and everyone will think I am normal, for they have no idea how much power I have. I was receiving messages on everything from conspiracies on how to save my planet, to how the most powerful president in the world was just a puppet and I was not going to ignore that. I was needed.

I had a purpose, and I was going to fulfil what I was put on earth for. I was within the hours when being and not being are not the same, I wanted to splatter and split wide this universe and I had to discard all illusions to enter the reality.

Freedom now meant keeping my thoughts to myself, never letting them know my ideas, for I realised my ideas were now dangerous to this world. If I expressed myself, I knew they would come for me in the night and drug me. I had to play the game and wait until my knowledge of what I needed to do was certain. I was only the student, I needed to know everything so that I could change the world for the better. I started to keep a notebook at this time.

I once showed her my notebooks, they were very elaborate, with diagrams of everything I had learnt. She tentatively asked me to explain them to her but I quickly realised she had no understanding of what was in them and remained silent.

So, like my thoughts, I hid them from prying eyes and continued working on them in the dead of the night when the Trinket men would come to me.

The Trinket men were strange I have to admit, in exchange for any knowledge they could give me, I had to collect trinkets for them. This could be broken jewellery, beads or tiny broken frames, in fact anything that was small and useful to them. I never asked them why they wanted the trinkets, it was just more about the universe and time.

Silently I was becoming a master and as yet nobody had cottoned on to the fact that their things were going missing. I was not going to swap her for anything, she was my beauty.

Her Voice

How can an ear break a heart?

Whenever I hear Debussy play it makes me want to cry, particularly the girl with the flaxen hair, the end high notes just make tears roll down my cheeks. How can an ear break a heart? Like a spear through the centre of me, it creates a desperate longing.

I do not know why this should be so but it is one of the most emotional pieces of music I have ever listened to. Mind, body and soul it enraptures overwhelming me with a deeply moving melancholy. I would like to put Debussy on repeat every day just to wake me from dreams and tell me that I am still alive. It is almost as though my soul knew this music first and tried to teach me something but I am still lacking the perception.

So, my eyes let my tears roll free, desperately trying to understand why this affects me so much. Maybe it was the time and the place when I first heard it but I cannot remember.

Like music, books always had a way of changing my life. John Fowles the Magus stayed with me deeply for a long time and Illusions by Jonathan Bach. Again, it may just have been the age I was when I first read or heard the music. But they had a profound influence on how I thought about things.

As I write this, I remember when he told me he was going away to find our life in his country. He wanted to take the girls with him and at that time within my sickness I said yes. Every single person I have ever spoke to disagreed with me, in fact my sister told me I was a terrible mother for allowing this. But nobody at that time understood or lived my life, so I can safely say nobody had a clue what they were talking about.

So it was. They all left me, I waved them off from the front garden as the sun teased the sky and night began to fall. It was the first time I noted that the moon bleeds if the sun bites her. Sitting in the garden I listened to the silence of my house, only hearing a lonesome bird cry, as a violet dusk bloomed.

Within that moment I realised everything returns to where it came from and so had my love.

They say change is as good as a rest, and for me it certainly was, I needed the space to be able to function as a human once more. My eldest child was being bullied at school and she also needed a change of her life. My youngest, I wanted her to be with her sister, as I always thought they would be good for each other. So, one day in early spring, they all left me, at this point I want to say I think it was the right thing for them all.

Do I think I will ever know for sure? No I do not.

For in that one fork in the road, all our lives divided without ever returning to the same.

His Voice

"The ones who are crazy enough to think they can change the world usually do."
– John MacAfee

When we arrived to my homeland, I felt illumined by the sun to the mysteries of life. My daughters loved the change of life and the space and freedom that was given to them but they were too young to notice the changes in me. I was growing stronger by the day.

My homeland is beautiful, the world is bluer here. At night the infinite sky shivers with stars rotating the sky, slowly, like a clockwork dream. Bougainvillea bursts around every corner, cobbled streets lead to the beach where the breakers heavy with brine in their hearts cast salt kisses on the sand.

I had now risen to another level and the Trinket men were giving me more and more tasks. I actually was more fearful at that point, for their voices became more forceful and their demands upon me left me scared that I could not complete the tasks.

They would usually come to me in silence through the television, I was now absolute certain nobody else could hear them but me. I had tried the question once with my wife when they had spoken to me in front of her. She looked blankly at me then bit her lip, I saw a small amount of blood slowly trickle from the side of her mouth and realised it was another thing to keep to myself.

But this certain night I found myself frozen in bed, the light was close to dying, darkness was erasing all traces from the room.

A Trinket man was in one corner of the room watching me, a face like all forgotten faces, but he had no eyelids or trace of a tongue, a translucent skin over fragile bones. He pleaded to me with the depths of his eyes, and in the air, I could perceive the absence of love.

As the bed and walls moved away from me so they could not hear what was said, I asked him if he was really there not breathing. He told me that he was no more than I think exists and asked me if I knew how it was just to be.

He only asked me what I already knew, someone somewhere set me free. His eyes never moved from my face and I wished I could move to hide under the covers.

He told me that the next day he would travel within my eyes and show me what road signs to take, he also told me I still did not understand a thing and his presence meant nothing more than I wished it to.

I watched the darkness accept him back into shadow, the room retained his odour which was unknown to me, the darkness made equal a rose and a bullet.

So, to the day I had been given a task. As daylight crept through the shutters and the shadows flew from the corners of the room, I watched the roofs at the edge of the fire and knew this was the day. The light now reflected on the wall makes words and symbols only I can understand. My inner clock was tick-tocking my mortality, I was not sure I knew any longer what day I was.

I called my daughters to welcome the brand-new day and told them we were taking a journey. When they asked me where, I told them it was a surprise, as at that point, I had no proper plan formulated, the Trinket man had not appeared.

As we began our journey, my mind now entered the race zone as I had become aware that I was now front-page news. I realised in the café when I was drinking my morning paper that people were eyeing me strangely and trying to hide the front cover of the newspaper from me.

This was a bad sign as the government were now going to try and kill me for my knowledge. I could not blame them as I had the secrets of the Universe inside my head.

I had to do what the Trinket men said, so I stopped at the first phone box to try and contact them. I had seen this done once in the film the *The Matrix* when the hero of the film attempted to stop reality. All I heard was the dead ring tone, so then I tried the next and the next and the next all were the same just a dead ring tone. I was becoming increasingly agitated as box after box had no way for me to escape.

I was trying to enter the change and calling out to everyone around me that I needed to leave this universe now but the Trinket men were not helping me. They had slid into the background and I could not hear their thoughts. I was just aware that I needed more than ever to escape this world right here right now. Without anyone to help I was now uncertain what to do but I knew that my assassins were right behind me and I needed to think logically to escape them.

So, I began circling roundabouts two or three times before deciding upon a direction. There were no thoughts behind this, I just needed to go quickly to a destination with a phone box that would allow me to escape. But as the Trinket men screamed silently inside me and my heart began thumping like a military drum, I found nowhere that I could connect.

We eventually ended up at land's end in that other country, my daughters seemed confused. So, trying to pull everything together, I slipped on my mask of control. I strained to listen to the Trinket man but all that was returned to me was a solitary nail being hammered into a cushion, silence.

The girls told me they were hungry as we had left without breakfast and it was now mid-afternoon. I remembered a restaurant I used to take my beauty to, the freshest fish eaten overlooking sparkling blue waters. The port where the fisherman landed was just next to the restaurant, so we climbed the steps and ate.

We ordered a huge sea bass caught that morning, with salad and we all had strawberries for dessert. The lunch was wonderful and my daughters chatted away, unaware of my morning, just content the drama for now, was over.

Under the weight of my eyelids and thick night, the Trinket man came back.

I saw a figure pass the windblown curtains, I trembled for what this might mean for me. Once more he sat in the corner, his eyes a vague notion of a glassy glaze, his thoughts hidden.

Once more I was frozen in bed, my mouth was open wide and I was already choking, I was terrified of the consequences of failure. I asked him why he did not help me, he replied that he was in front of me but that I was staring at the door behind him.

With a certain sadness to his tone, he told me that I had failed the task of the day. I asked him what that meant for me, he shrugged his shoulders and said it means nothing more than you wish it to. I apologised for my failure and told him I was terrified that the government now wanted to kill me. Once more he shrugged his shoulders and said if you wish them to, they will.

Dissolving back into the darkness, he left once more his elusive perfume in the air.

I had failed, I could not believe it, I could not fail, it was imperative that I managed to complete the tasks. I left the house intention-less and walked for miles along the clifftops towards a stairway that led to the sea.

The world did not change, it was still business as usual but the darkness now flowed between two possibilities. A hooded Trinket man repeatedly corrected me as within this black hole now opening in front of me, he opened up his cloak to shield us from sight.

My cigarette spraying a circle of sparks in the wind, I heard the sound of dogs barking upon the clifftops. In the distance someone was playing an accordion then suddenly there was silence all around me. My mind went to a film clip I once saw, 'Club Silencio' from the film *Mulholland Drive.*

It was as though when I watched that movie something inside me barred the doors to yesterday and tomorrow. It was an insomniac night, shaping bags under the eyes. The singer glides to the footlights under shadow of night as the curtains of her pupils slowly rise. A single spasm catches her, sadness enraged, an almond-eyed chimera, neurotically bright. As the sound of her voice echoes inside, you sink into the ethereal, paralysed by the sound of her singing. Then as the clock agrees upon the cracked hour, she collapses and you realise that everything you had seen was an illusion.

For the voice continues its powerful rendition of crying whilst she lies on the floor not moving. Two stagehands rush to pick her body up off the floor and all that is left is the haunting voice still singing.

These thoughts in my fevered mind punctured the fabric of my reality.

.

I split apart and walked towards the water's edge. My story now so confused, my distress as clear as a bell, erase the story or live in the pain. I wanted to go back to listen to the pebbles and eat peaches and oranges.

Gazing down into the water, I see my face staring back at me, letting my body droop I start to go slack. All behind me and under me was now empty, and I began to fall, when suddenly a vein in the bitter sea broke and I was pushed back with an almighty force. I swept the sand to the four corners of the wind and watched as each breath I gasped; the Trinket man breathed with me.

I heard cries coming from the clifftops but their voices rumbled far in the distance. Under my skin the moon becomes alive and disorientated, lost in the silence of dust, my mind in the stream became a bright white silence.

The next thing I was aware of was, I was in a hospital corridor waiting for sentence to be passed. Lying on a trolley in a lime green walled corridor, I decided I should leave.

Escaping in my pyjamas I wandered through the city of the old town. Headlights passed by me then descended into a void, under cover of dark I walked inside my shadow. My legs carried me into the maze of cobbled streets which were harsh under my bare feet. The hot pavements sparked a flint underfoot.

I could see bystanders staring at me watching this tragic illusion called I, and in this sprawling city of people procession, they cynically viewed my destiny. I had become the anonymous passer-by, an unbroken chain of dawns in my mind, my eyes still making a new world each day.

Lost in my memories I commenced to rewind, I heard a window open but I know that it is not her, for she has slipped into my nightmares. I can see her walk but someone else walks her footsteps. I am burnt and probed by the spectator's stares, two tired legs walking this city.

I curl up on the pavement under curious skies, feeling a vague sense of desperation at not being illumined by the Trinket man, to the mystery of reality.

When I woke, I found I was back on a trolley in the corridor of the hospital. They transferred me to another hospital that they said specialised in my type of illness which made me laugh. How could all these intelligent people not understand that I was not ill? Where were the bonds of my life, my mirrors and my days, how can you escape one's own mind?

The next day her parents arrived to save me, they booked a ticket for my flight home to be with her and promised to look after my daughters.

The following night I was in England lying on our kitchen floor at three in the morning begging her to open the church for me. Under my eyelids, eternity was flickering, whilst I was caught in temporal boundaries, my mind was an explosion of stars somewhere. I just wanted to make things logical.

Her Voice

"One must still have chaos in oneself to be able to give birth to a dancing star."
– Friedrich Nietzsche

Going nowhere in the timeless now, my mirror reflects the songs of despair. Exhausted, I went around to a neighbour whom I knew had the keys for the church, with a heart as big as the world he agreed to meet us there. This man will never know how much he helped me that evening, thank you was not enough.

How weird that in the darkest hours of the night you begin to wonder about everything, whether or not you can make it until sunrise, will our fragile minds now buckle under the pressure?

Waiting outside for him to exit, I gazed at the moon unbreathing. As he rippled past me with the faintest murmur, I saw his dilated eyes had lost their fire. Mute and orphaned silence swam around me, he hid an enigma code, a new language for despair. I could feel the heaviness of his tired uneven steps, he smelt of sadness and tobacco. Threads inside me unfolded and my spirit sighed.

He stood in the freezing air of a winter's night pulling my heart out of my chest. His almond eyes created for love and faith had chosen a dim light bulb over daylight. If I could find my way back through memory's mirrors I would reach for the chapter of simple miracles, see once more the jewels in your teardrops. You have passed through waves into rocks and this winter has wrapped you in snow.

I asked him why we were going to church at this hour of the night.

He told me that as he lay on a stretcher in the corridor awaiting help in the foreign hospital, a vision came to him. He had realised that the nursing staff were placing people in front of him so that he could heal them. It was the first time that he thought his special purpose was to heal people. I cried when he said that he was special and our kind neighbour who had opened the church was wonderful to us both.

We sat in the church waiting for him to talk, but not a word came from his lips, a peace came over him and he wanted to leave. Without explanation, all of the drama had gone, he was ready for sleep.

Calm, we left the church to a starry night of lights twinkling at us, and it was his first mention of Sirius, I presumed he meant the brightest star, now I am not so sure. Cold now with age and winter, we turned to face a black frosty night with grey hair. The moonlight fell everywhere, no special place, we looked at the starlight that once was, yet upon reaching our eyes it had already ceased to be. I realised then that in this eternity we stand nowhere.

The following day he was sectioned once more.

This time a deep torture was carved into my soul, I just wanted to keep my shadow safe and keep sane. Sometimes I caught myself weeping over a distant life. I used cigarettes like the lollipops of my childhood, my clouds flooding the air. Walking through the doors of my bitterness, I howled to the Gods at the hand they had dealt me. I felt like I was trapped inside the moon with my own chaotic imagery.

I became a lonely woman looking in the mirror, thinking tomorrow will break and I will be a ghost.

My children continued their education abroad, whilst I sat in front of the windows of my house, waiting for the breath of the world to come once more.

He had through our time together, drilled himself inside me and stood right behind my eye, every thought I had was of him and that he would get better.

Now I sat on the quivering scales of the past sunk inside myself, inside my own matter, trying to listen to the footsteps of my dreams. Knowing that they were long gone and every day was going to be me waiting for the bitter sea to break. The hope of ever seeing his smile again had turned the hours into thieves, and here I was on the edge of a knife blade in the labyrinth of his shade.

But I can tell you with hindsight how much I had at that point underestimated him.

When my daughters returned from abroad, he was still in hospital, this time it was over a year. They did not want to come home but home they did come.

Her Voice

"The mystery of human existence lies not in just staying alive, but in finding something to live for."
– Fyodor Dostoyevsky

From the place I am in now, I did go back home once in a while to see him.

When I arrived after so many years away from England, I was amazed by how green it was. Also, how friendly the people were. I realised how much I missed the language and the humour of the people, the soul food, and the beautiful English countryside. I was reminded of Robert Browning's classic poem *Home-Thoughts from Abroad*, I had truly in my despair forgotten how beautiful England was.

Before I went to my house, I decided to take a long detour across the fields that I usually took with my dog. The land had not changed one bit as I walked over the bridge across a babbling brook. The earth still smelt of frost and musty winter even though Spring had arrived. The days now drew their curtains between four and five. I could see across the wintry landscape, a group of birds huddling under a roof.

I remembered so many happy times playing pooh sticks with my daughters. Continuing onward I passed the old manor house walking further into the woods ending up near the train track.

A memory rush came to me of my dog we called Lobo, who when he heard the train rumbling towards us, pricked up his ears in anticipation of what was to come. As the train hurtled down the track, he would then chase the train barking until it was no longer in reach. He used to run back panting, so happy, thinking he had chased the train away. An inner smile warmed me inside.

I decided to take a short cut back as the light was now close to dying. The day had grown tired of chasing the night and the sun was beginning to set. My feet were toasty warm, slippered in nostalgia, as I made a zig-zag across the fields towards the lights of the village.

When I entered the house, as it was never locked, he lay on the sofa, a beer in hand, which was now his normal routine. Our beautiful home in which I had taken such pride was now destroyed.

The worn-out house now rested on time, darkness infiltrating the floors and walls. Black mould was creeping through the house as if it was reading our minds. All the kitchen cabinets had been kicked in at some point and nothing no longer worked. All my beautiful plants were long dead and the house was infested with neglect.

I wanted to cry but realised there was no home here now, it was an empty shell just like him and I. I wanted to cry, but what good would it have done?

We hugged as usual as I entered, then I adopted my usual chair, curling up inside it, like an old friend's hug. He was watching some soap of the day, so I sat and gazed at the ruination of a life so blessed, whilst he steadily opened can after can of beer.

He would only speak if I spoke to him, crossing and uncrossing his legs, his breathing laboured and his fingers steadily drumming against his chest. His mouth when it moved did not seem to belong to him anymore.

The voices between us did not connect, they were thin and sparse like needles. Our promises shattered like discarded crystals, as behind silent masks we flickered a non-life.

It was hard not to compare the sound of our grandmother clock to chatter, warmth and the sun smiling bright. I tried not to compare anything to anything at all I just wanted to get through the visit intact. I decided to count the passing of the days here, my fingers forgetting the sweetness as my blood sours.

As the clock struck early hours I went to bed, the daydreams of meeting my old friend were crushed. We have hidden our dead bodies in the cellar and built bricks so that they cannot cry out. I tried to search for some resemblance of the person that he had been but there was nothing to grasp, only a shadow.

How had our happiness passed us by so quickly? He was only 39 years old when the sickness entered him. Corners of our dreams take me on repeat to the falls and clouds of our beginning where fate had chosen a dead-end street.

Resting my head on the edge of my pillow I lay weeping over a distant life. He had made a nest in his emptiness, full of beer and mindless TV. I had made my nest in another country, full of vodka and loneliness.

The following morning the dawn dyed the world elephant grey. A soft light settled on the dust in the rooms but the air was stale inside. I opened the windows and the wind swept through the bedroom, so I dressed myself in the morning breeze. Seeing once more the destruction and smashed spaces I suggested we go into the garden and talk.

I made us coffee, hot, strong, sweet and carried it to the white plastic table outside. We sat on two white plastic chairs wobbling on the uneven concrete surrounded by a jungle of overgrown plants. The lawn was full of tiny mushrooms which had made their home in the long grass and weeds. Scents filled the air from a clutch of dawn's dwelling amongst the wild honeysuckle. Where once this space was mown grass and neat shrubs it was now unrecognisable. Caught inside a cobweb spell, I realised how could I think I would ever be free?

Spring had started to wander through the ignored garden, I remembered so well how I had bought and tended to the plants. The honeysuckle had taken over and made a curve in one side of the fencing. The back fence was now destroyed but the firs beyond this still gave the garden privacy. It was then that I began to notice certain odd things arranged on the lawn.

I left my seat and went closer to inspect what was hiding in the long grass. The first thing that had caught my eye was a buddha, he was sitting peacefully with his legs crossed next to a bronze angel cherub, a tiny money spider running across his nose. The cherub was holding a vase with which to put plants in and next to the cherub was a plate of rice. In front of the cherub was a knife driven into the ground with its sharp end, next to that an ordinary alarm clock and last but not least a torch. The items had been arranged into two rows with three items per row.

On the washing line behind me he had placed his national flag between the two poles and another pole was off to the left with another washing line connected to it. I wondered at first if it was a game of some sort but could not imagine what the game could be.

His answer when it came from softly behind me; answered all my questions.

The Buddha and the angel were there to protect him, should anything bad happen, the rice was to give him sustenance on his journey. The knife was simply for protection, the alarm clock was so he could tell the time and the torch was for light in the darkness. There was also a yellow football sat on the grass to the side of these, which he said was to remind him that the sun is always there, every day, even if masked by the clouds of this country.

I nodded my head slowly, understanding how all this made sense to him, I asked what the flag was for and he replied it was to show everyone his identity and who he was. Realising that the washing lines were probably also part of this, I asked him if he could explain their positions to me.

His reply shocked me, as he told me he had invented a time travel machine, and that he was preparing for his journey. I smiled nervously as I realised that he was disconnected, then sat and let him talk to me and show me his notebooks. As I read, I realised that his mind once again had set sail for a sea of stars, he was neither here or there, a lost balloon in a forest of trees.

Once more the voices between us did not connect as if they sucked the light from eyes now dead. Prayers now crumpled between our fingers each in search of a remedy to make the cure. But there was no cure, and I could have cried, but what good would it have done?

No longer after all those years did, we understood one other.

The following day he disappeared.

I woke to silence, but this was usual, he never appeared before ten. I made myself some toast from the bread I had brought and a coffee. The small fridge was packed full of pizzas, one for each day of the week, all salami and cheese.

The previous few years it had been an obsession with sardines but he had obviously decided pizzas were now his food for the day and he never wavered, he ate them every day without fail. There were Danish pastries for breakfast and a huge amount of chocolate biscuits in the tins as a variety. I spread some butter I had brought onto my toast, took my breakfast to the table and commenced to look at my Kindle.

Only once afternoon had begun did I realise he had still not emerged. I tentatively knocked on his door and called his name but no answer. Something did not seem right.

As I opened the door, I viewed the place where he usually slept, which in happier times was my youngest daughter's room. He had saved our bedroom for me and my mother had been and changed the sheets. His room was black with mould and his sheets black from not being washed. The bed looked like it had not been slept in but this was not unusual as the bed was never made. His new shoes were missing that we had brought yesterday when we went shopping.

We had woken up yesterday and decided to go shopping together, breakfast was as strange as ever with him telling me about God and the devil talking to him.

I asked him what they would talk about but he glossed over the subject and just told me that I would like God's wife. When I asked why, he simply replied that she was very kind to him, and that she liked me. When I asked him about the devil, he said that he was not a nice person and just suggested unkind things to him. I let it go as I could see my prying was beginning to irritate him.

I drove us both into town in my hired car, the music playing was the Gypsy Kings that we always used to play in the restaurant. And so, at last we connected and were both tapping our feet and singing Bamboleo at the tops of our voices all the way to the shops.

We brought him a new pair of shoes and a dress for our granddaughter. We went to his favourite pub and he got quite drunk! He loved the all-day breakfasts in the pub and would sit and eat everything put in front of him along with pints of lager.

I needed to do more shopping so left him drinking and went to buy more. He made me laugh and I made him smile, we connected the dots. Holding his arm to stop him from swaying, we made our way back to the car giggling and talking with abandon, we had had a good day.

On the way back he told me that I was his star in the sky, he told me to go to look for the star in the sky that connected us...

I hung around the house for another few hours then decided to go for a walk, when I came home, he had returned. I told him that I was worried, he said that I needn't be and that he was fine.

It was at that moment that I noticed his new shoes, the backs of his shoes were so worn down as if he had had them for ten years. I said for him to look at his new shoes and he shrugged.

I asked if he had been walking the universe in them, he winked and smiled then went to lie on the sofa.

His Voice

"Taking crazy things seriously is a serious waste of time."
– Haruki Murakami

I need to tell you about the barbecue and my country playing football. She had long left at this time. I invited all my brothers and father to come over to my house to watch the world cup and enjoy an evening of fun, drinks and football. It was for once a warm summer's evening in England.

It was my country's night to shine, we were the champions and oh how I have always loved football. I purchased the beers and food, supplied the atmosphere and we were all having a great time. Up until my neighbour thought we were being too loud.

Now my neighbour has always been a bitch, she has hated my children playing, my dog barking and my different culture ever since we moved next door to her. She is one of those people that never has a good word to say about anyone.

From the time we moved into our dream house she has put complaint after complaint against us for such stupid things. As an example, if my children used the back fence to get to the children's park or if my dog barked after ten o clock. Everything and anything she could find her way to moan about she would. If we had any parties that lasted after ten o'clock, she would call the police, she drove me mad with her constant whining.

So, we must go now to this night, my family and I were having a lively football world cup party, our country had played so well and we were all rejoicing in the fact we had won.

The bitch decided that she would spoil any fun we were deriving from this, she had made her mind up. Firstly, she asked me to turn down the music, I immediately resented this.

All of our lives she has tried to press her will onto us, this old lady believes that her right is above mine. For one night only, a barbecue on an important social event for me and she has to try to destroy that, is that just or fair?

I would argue from a utilitarian standpoint that no, from the logic that greater numbers are for the greater good. Why should one person try to spoil seven people's enjoyment? In my mind that is not correct. Why in certain situations do the minority have the right to spoil the pleasure of the majority?

Our government has been so utilitarian on their other ideas of paternalism, why on this point do they back down and make an individual's rights, above the rights of the majority? It makes no sense to me.

Enraged as I was with her that night, I screamed and I screamed, until I was hoarse. I said to my family that I would kill her, for what she was doing to me and that was taking away any happiness or freedom to enjoy myself. Now I know, I didn't mean it literally, I would not hurt a fly but this stupid bitch without any thought for me called the police.

I smashed everything I could find, from the glasses, to the bottles, to the kitchen cupboards, my rage knew no bounds. I kicked in every kitchen cupboard just to release what was going on inside. But I never once went over to her side of the fence and tried to kill her. So why did this old bitch call the police, did she really think I would go in the dead of the night and murder her, or did she just want me put away?

If the police came to your door, I am sure they would just ask you to turn the music down, but oh no, not me.

I had run into the police before on numerous occasions, I knew their powers. For example, there was one time when I wanted drivers to be more cautious and aware so I would step out into traffic just to let them know that it was possible, if they were not paying attention that they could hit someone. Most of them like lunatics gave me the V sign or angrily berated me from their cars. I was at a loss to see why they could not understand, I was trying to change the world for them and help them wake up.

I was also given a job as a chef at a famous supermarket and believed that the government wanted to introduce health and safety laws so that they could control us. The longer I was there, the more I believed that this was true, so many rules and regulations, how on earth had previous generations survived?

So, I decided to raise a bit of anarchy by being dirty, just simple things like putting food onto dirty plates, not washing my hands, the list could go on. I felt I was battling for the people, I did not want this government mind control anymore, I wanted people to wake up and see that all the nanny state was doing was trying to control us.

This continued until the day I was found out, and I could not open my eyes. They summoned me to the management, where I stood in front of them with my eyes closed and them pleading for me to open my eyes. Which I absolutely would not do.

I did not want to look at the sheep of the government, I did not want to listen to their words. So, eyes closed, I stood there blind and speechless until they were so agitated, they were nearly at screaming point.

The more they kept telling me to open my eyes the more my eyes seemed to be glued together. They had absolutely no idea how to deal with me. It was only when I heard the sirens outside the door, I knew once again the police had come for me. I think I went to my alternative home at the hospital for six months that time.

Another time was when I decided to go on holiday, it does not matter where I was, some people will tell you I was in Cumbria but I am certain I was in York. I mean did it really matter to anyone?

I went on holiday, they say I was in Cumbria, I say I was in York. I booked into a hotel, but when I got into bed, I could hear the shadows whisper.

The Trinket man then told me there was a fire. I panicked and ran through the hotel breaking every glass of each fire alarm. Once more I was arrested by the police and placed in a cell until they realised their mistake. I was no criminal, and if anybody had bothered to check with me, I could have told them that. Within a few hours I was back in hospital.

So back to the night my neighbour had called the police, they came to my door, called me by name and put me into the back of the police car. Once more I was taken to my second home. I have to say that the police I dealt with were always very nice to me. I think deep down they did not want to spoil my fun, but they do have a job to do.

A throw away comment that anyone on this planet makes on a daily basis had suddenly made me public enemy number one. Is this the stigma of mental illness?

Yes, it is in my book, a person without any supposed mental problems would be advised to turn the music down. It would not even be thought an issue that they had a problem with the neighbour for spoiling their fun. But not for me I was now a crazy, a danger to society, I had said that I would kill someone, nothing in my nature would have done that, I was now classed differently.

But this cannot be verified with objective tests, mental illness cannot stand up to scientific scrutiny. There is no specific treatment or predictable outcome as in the case of cancer or a broken leg.

You hear every day people threatening other people but we all know it is just hot air, it isn't real, why when I speak, is it deemed literal? If everything everyone says is true, we would all be in jail, or sued for slander, or libel.

They say I do not live in reality, mine is a fictional world, but it is only others that make that assumption, my world is as real to me as yours. Who therefore has the right to say what is real and what is fiction?

I have not a violent bone in my body, everyone who describes my nature says I am soft, a pacifist, I don't hold with violence. So why now, am I thought to be someone with harmful intent? This does not make sense to me.

All of my life, I had only ever been involved in one fight and that was between my brother and his friend. They were arguing one night outside a nightclub and suddenly started throwing punches at each other. I stepped in to make them stop, my brother swung and hit me square in the mouth and I lost my front teeth.

The dentist did a fantastic job and I had a lovely set of new false front teeth. But this proves that in the whole of my life I have never been involved with violence, I was actually the peacemaker.

From that one complaint, and the Doctor's losing patience with me for not taking the tablets, I was now faced with something far more serious.

We now go to the night I called my wife and let her know that they were going to take my mind away by injection. I did not have a leg to stand on this, it had been ordered by the courts. Remembering once they had told her to sleep with a base-ball bat under the bed, just in case, I knew they thought I was dangerous.

She knew what that call would mean to my life, she knew that what I had said would make me a zombie. This was the most profoundly disturbing, harrowing moment of my life, as I was no longer being treated like a normal person. I had not done anything to that day to harm any person, let alone myself.

I was being treated like an animal, forcibly injected, as some judge in some tribunal had decided I was a danger.

I was in the court that day, and tried to defend myself against the white coats, but nobody would believe me that I was not mentally ill. These strangers, who had no idea who I was or what my personality was like.

For it is true with mental illness, strangers are allowed to judge you and make you a prisoner if they see fit, without a proper trial. Given the fact I was harmless and had no intention of killing myself or anyone else, why had I to take tablets or be forcibly injected when I was enjoying my life?

Some might have found me strange but is that a crime?

How many conspiracy theorists are out there, protesting with crazy ideas about a flat earth, a vaccine, fake moon landings, terror attacks. Yet these are not seen as delusions, they are seen as a human need for control, understanding and belonging. They seem to be a basic human need, to have control over a reality that is confusing or unpredictable.

Tell me what is the difference in me wanting control and understanding over my reality?

I personally cannot see any difference.

I saw their huddled heads nodding feverishly, what do we do with the wounded mind? Passing their sentence ignoring my cries for what is right they looked at me with pitiful eyes.

As my scream echoed around the tribunal, the voices sensing my distress did not speak. I turned to stone under their gazes caught inside their cobweb spell of lies. I see her green eyes sparkling through the glass, like Persephone before me, a decision has been made. My tortured mind kicks at the fait accompli, how could I think I would ever be free to follow my path?

After that I was numb for she did not come to rescue me. My life was about to change forever and she was no longer there.

This was the first time they had forcibly injected me; my mind had now been left to this delusion we call life.

Inside the room where they prepared the injection, I could hear the Trinket men in the shadows whispering to me. I stepped out of my mind to the depths of despair as the light darkened under the sobbing tree. There was simply nothing else I could do but to accept my fate.

As a zombie I now had a free life but as a zombie what was I to do with this life now granted to me? Walk the walk, talk the talk, but without any emotion to back me up, how am I supposed to survive?

I am too afraid of death to ever commit suicide, so I am left in a half state somewhere between coma and living, which is essentially a half-awake feeling that cannot have emotion.

So, to the night of the injection, moonlight fell everywhere, no special place. I was destined for a hell that was not of my making bathing in the rivers of some false light. I was about to enter an intention-less void where love is not truth and truth is not love.

Imagine your life without emotion, what would you do, would you get out of bed? It is like a life without weather, every day turns into bland, you do not care if a loved one is ill or worried. You are blocked from your feelings; it is like eating food without the taste.

So, in essence that was what happened to me and I spend my days now lying on the sofa unable to think, just watching the TV in front of me. That great pacifier, the brain numbing thing in front of me, is this a life?

I began to remember what I had been taught, with all the books I had read from science, religion and philosophy. There was a way out of this, even though everyone thought, I was now pacified and not a danger, I was not going to live like this anymore.

I was determined to get away from this mind-numbing prison simply by my energy. My reality was not this, I had seen universes in my brain, I was not sure how I could reach them, but even though everyone now thought they had made me into a zombie, I knew this was not reality. For reality is your energy, not this physicality. I began to summon with the little strength I had left in me the Trinket men. This is where in secret my adventure started.

Her Voice

"Within the sunset of our dissolution, half of ourselves we lost."

When I went to visit him after he had started the injections, the change was so huge it literally took my breath away. No longer did his thoughts race through life, his sparkling eyes had ceased to dance. It was as though his mind had fallen through some trap door and he sat in a place between what is and what is not, in nowhere and everywhere under a spell.

We hugged as I entered as usual, it was the lack of eye contact that rendered past to the present, nothing reverberated. All life in the house had disappeared inside an empty glass. I tried lifting the present to the past as I thundered down the tunnel of my life time with him. His answers were mono-syllabic, the warmth of his voice and smile had faded. It was as if all the words from the dictionary had flown away. My tears wanted to spill onto the carpet but what good would that have done?

He went to sit in the lounge on his sofa which had the indents of his body where he lay every day, flickering a non-life. I took the armchair I always used to use and we watched television. He slowly drank beer after beer after beer but nothing was said.

We had grandchildren by this time and the following morning they came to see us. I realised then that all the Kit Kats and chocolates in the house were brought for them.

Each night I slept in our once bedroom was like a jagged edge. I spelt out prayers in the blackness, wishes upon wishes, prayers upon prayers, all useless. These were our lives now.

Each night I sat across from myself, to confront myself face to face, rocking myself in my damaged boat, his love always sitting behind my eyes.

As a bird knows its own tree so do I, comfort is where I continue to go. I just wanted a welcome that was heartfelt, I was now hardened also by the scars that had thickened with each mask I portrayed. He had pulled my petals off one by one until like the stars we were paralysed and I could no longer fly to the moon.

He then asked me how do the dead live. I replied that I did have an answer to this, although I knew my answer, but did not want to tell, you will remember I have already told you how this can happen. He shrugged his shoulders and said without waiting for an answer:

"Know that the dead live by a thing called love."

But as much torture as this was for me, I kept going back.

Everyone saw me drinking too much, choosing the wrong people, but nobody saw the damage that was done, that was up to me.

But how mistaken were my words? Not one person understood us. My children, my family, they all thought I was another person. Yet I was the same person I had always been, only difference being, the change had now affected their lives.

When you invite others into your problem that is when things start to change.

My husband and I were the only two people left on this planet that understood what the change was.

We continued feeling like we were chess pieces on life's boardgame.

It was very hard for me to get him to open up as he did not trust me anymore. So much had been passed between us, that we were definitely in different universes.

When I first left the home that we had brought and lived in all our lives, I only moved a few houses away to stay with my mum and dad, that way I could still keep an eye on my daughters but the pressure was off, having to deal with the illness on a day-to-day basis.

But I found this was not the case, as he never saw this as a separation, he would still call me at all hours, during night and day. My work suffered and my colleagues were understanding to a point but then told me that I had to switch my mobile off. I tried to explain to them my situation, but they were right, they were paying me to work. I was at this point breaking down in every way. So, when I did not answer he would turn up at my mum's house with something or everything that was bothering him.

My mind is now going to another knife incident where he was threatening. He sat in the kitchen with yet another knife between us, this one he placed onto the table and we sat down. He accused me of spying on him. Oh, how do you possibly reason with someone in a different reality to you?

He told me that he knew it was me, as he could see the blue light flashing, and was aware of what I was doing. I tried to explain to him that this was just our neighbour's burglar alarm but he told me that he knew how clever I was and he wanted me to stop spying.

I looked at the knife, then at him, his face agitated in the silence. I swore to him that it was not me. I went over and held him. As he broke down, I removed the knife from the table and slipped it into one of the drawers behind me. He did not even realise what he had done, maybe he just wanted a cuddle.

Yet again the stresses and no one believing what was happening to me played hard with my emotions.

I did realise at this point that there was no escape, I was bound to him and he was bound to me and no matter where I was, he would enter my head.

So that night at Mum's house I was watching the shopping channel, which by the way, not once before or since have I ever looked at this sort of TV. This night I distinctly remember seeing a ring of stones and diamonds. I could not tell you if they were real or not or why I was sat there watching that shit. But there I was watching this beautiful ring in front of my eyes and thinking I needed peace.

With no thought at all I went into the kitchen to my dad's medicine cabinet. To say he had tablets was underestimating; what was before me, it was like a pharmacist's heaven with so many pills. I did not even to bother to look at the tablets, I just started to take them with alcohol.

This is hard for me to tell as I am so ashamed of myself. After I had took this stupid cocktail, I rang my sister and told her what I had done. She immediately said she would call an ambulance.

How stupid I feel now, how much did I put on others that night, in a drink fuelled state. Oh, if I could ever change one whole night, it would be this one where I cannot think of this without cringing inside.

The hospital quite rightly had no time for me, I was play acting, this was no real attempt, just a tortured addled brain. I now hang my head with shame as to how I manipulated people who save lives, and my sister, to witness my dramas.

In search of a remedy to make a cure, I had entered an abyss. I had tried escaping the birth of old sunsets but my life had switched out our light. I wanted to obliterate old versions of me and no longer live as a reflection of the past.

Because when everything is pain in your life, you need a way out, your judgement gets so clouded that it becomes nearly impossible to choose your route and just sometimes in your drunk confused brain, you split from yourself and do stupid things.

But finally, I managed to leave, thinking this would be an end to my sorrow, oh, how wrong I was. The past constantly dogged my footsteps, I was as free as a bird in a cage.

His Voice

"When we remember we are all mad, the mysteries
disappear and life stands explained."
– Mark Twain

The day I disappeared from the house, and re-entered with
my shoes worn down, this was the first true gift the Trinket
men had given me.

Before this I can remember them showing me through
the rear window in a taxi to Manchester, Rome burning. It
scared the shit out of me.

In front of me there was Manchester and Piccadilly
station which was where I was heading on my infamous
holiday when I set all the fire alarms off. I turned around to
view the rear screen and behind me was Rome and its
Colosseum on fire. How could this be?

My wife and I had been to Rome many years ago, it was
one of our most romantic times together, of which I can say
there were many. I had always had a love for the Colosseum
as I grew up on Gladiator type films. So, was my mind at
this point trying to warn me?

Was this a warning that all my fires had been burnt with her and now I needed to look to the future and not the past? The answer came suddenly, it was staring me directly in the face, the future contained the present, I had turned around in that taxi and could see the past hurtling along behind me to escape this empty present.

It was now so easy to see what had to be done, I needed to escape my present reality and begin to alter the past. For those were the days of my life, I had nothing left to live for, if I could not find my way back to them.

I started to apply everything the Trinket men had spoken to me about and all that I had read in the books about quantum theory and philosophy. I had to alter my life for I knew that she was lost in some foreign country without me.

This was not an easy thing to do, in fact most people would say it was impossible, but they did not have my life's experiences. Nobody had any clue what was in my mind. So, I set about trying to turning my reality to the past.

So, to the day that I disappeared.

With something new to try, I woke much earlier than my usual hour, I decided to put my headphones on and listen to Debussy. There is something eerie in his music that made it fit the mood I was in. Walking out into the garden to the things she had mocked, I saw my energy in each of things as a ray of hope.

I knew that if I reversed everything that had happened, we could finally make it.

As the music vibrated in my ears, I concentrated on the vibrations in the garden.

The Trinket men had told me what to look for and I truly believed this would work. I, who had seen the past of Rome burning; I, who had seen how Jesus had healed the sick; I, who understood the crazy people who were sane; I, who knew that what people called crazy, was simply a person in another reality to their own and I knew that this belief would carry me forward and take me to the life I wanted back.

I had already practiced on her. Once, I managed to make the reality around her dissolve when she was in the bathroom. She tried to touch the tiles but was so frightened she did not move and thought it was a dream. She stayed sitting like a stone for at least two hours until everything returned to normal.

The second time I actually managed to alter the room she was sleeping in so that she woke up in the other reality with everything changed. What I did not realise at this time was how to stay there. This is why when I went away with my girls and tried to follow the Trinket men's orders specifically, I was using the telephone boxes for their energy to escape the reality I had created to try and make her awake.

I made an oath to the Trinket men to never reveal their secrets. But my advice is to look into the light for whatever you wish to discover.

As once more the afternoon settled around me, I lifted the weight of the present to the past watching as the mist of rain began to erase my view. The room is exhausted by my empty glass so I go and fetch some more whisky from the cupboard. I am grounded now in the clouds of the rain, echoes of the past now spin and reflect their answer to me.

As the rain eased and the clouds opened their curtains, I made my way into the garden. I sat upon my wobbly plastic chair and tried to find her. There she is, the drunken poet, chatting to strangers in some foreign café. I knew she could not see me so I tried to see the young woman I met, the girl with the light in her eyes. I needed to teach my little sparrow how to fly again, for all the storms have clipped her wings, she is a changeling now substituted every ten or more years.

Leaving her, to concentrate my mind, I strained to let go of thought.

Needless to say, within an hour of my concentrating on my breathing and the vibrations of sounds that surrounded me, I suddenly left the garden!

I found myself in the wind fully fledged, so I blew on the clock of a dandelion and time dispersed through fields of gold. Moving the sky to one side I reached out as onto wings of eternity and began to fly. I emerged through a pinprick of light and with my torch in my hand I searched for home. In the deep midnight hum of the universe, minds in the window glass echo and reflect as I chased the wind through empty streets.

My flight touched the colours of the sky and I sensed the darkness beyond. I set about searching for a guide like our star whose fire might nurture this aching for the past.

Gazing downwards I saw ice smothering the roses in the long-forgotten garden, fairy lights sprinkled around the house, I knew this was a Christmas past. Oh, how I wanted to stop there now, dive into the memory and stay.

What was I in this moment, the light that floats or the darkness itself? I flew through day and night, both in time and above it. I was everywhere and nowhere in a timeless now, just being. Whatever time, is, I will always return as it is always there, waiting for us to dive into a snapshot.

Are you reading this and thinking I am crazy; this could never have happened? Yes, I can see your point of view, it must be quite hard to understand. But it did happen and my reality is the only one that counts to me.

But I knew there were many things to do yet to make her believe that I was not crazy and that this was simply not our lives.

Now I just needed to wake her up and realise that I was not out of my mind!

So, I asked her to come and visit me as I needed her help. She booked a flight a week later and walked through the door as she had done a thousand times with a hug and a smile.

As the day broke free of the morning, an icy wind whipped the leaves through the street. The rain is shaking and shouting at the windows, erasing the view beyond the glass, and there she is!

I asked her if we could go away for a few days just the two of us. We decided upon Wales where we had gone so many moons ago. This was just perfect for me, a natural environment to connect to the past.

We set out on our road trip the following day with her making a packed lunch of bread with chorizo and tomato and cheese, one of my all-time favourite pizzas. She had packed a few Peroni beers, crisps and two Danish pastries and we were off on our adventure.

We were now going back to the photograph of the wall. We hardly talked on the journey, we just listened to various discussions on the radio, which made us laugh, get angry and cry at the same time. After too many debates and discussions, I inserted a cassette and good to go, we sang the Gypsy Kings all the way to Wales.

The car now appointed with music slipped into the night and at dawn we arrived at our destination.

Her Voice

"To feel the love of people whom we love is a fire that feeds our life."
– Pablo Neruda

So here we were back inside the photograph that used to hang on the wall. The past was now the present.

The exception was our grey hair, larger physiques and personalities.

We booked into the same hotel overlooking the wall that we had stayed in all those years ago. His laboured breathing and shuffling steps contrasted to the handsome man that had told me he loved me so many years ago.

We decided to share the same room with twin beds this time. As we entered the room, I asked him if he would take a bath. His hygiene was not the greatest, just like our once beautiful house, he had let himself go in so many ways.

I looked inside his suitcase whilst he was taking a bath, to see if had brought any of his tablets. A stupid thing to have done as that was the last thing he would bring.

I began to wonder when he had his last injection but had no way of knowing this.

He came out of the bathroom a wonder, gone was his Santa Claus beard, his habitual moustache was still there. He had shaved his head from a long hippy style to a buzz cut and clipped all his nails.

The transformation was incredible, we went down for dinner arm in arm. He pulled out my chair for me to sit down. Allowing him to lead, he asked for the menu and chose a bottle of wine that both of us loved. We both decided on pepper steak with fried potatoes and green beans. This had always been a favourite of ours.

The conversation did not flow but I could still make him smile with my observations. Luckily the restaurant had a duet who kept us entertained and as we listened to the music, we held hands across the table. At the end of the dinner and the performance we went outside to walk along the wall.

The moon and stars were out and he asked me once more if I could spot our star. This time it took no effort to understand what he was saying. It was literally the brightest star in the sky and he asked me to send a wish to the star.

I wished at that moment to send the clocks back in time, change our futures and never let the change affect our lives.

Once done with my wish he seemed content and told me he was tired and would like to go to bed. I asked him if he wished me to accompany him to the room but he told me he was fine going up alone.

So, I went into town and brought from an off-licence there, a bottle of vodka and some diet coke. Sneaking a glass out, from the now closed bar of the hotel, I poured myself a drink and said cheers to the moon.

I sat alone in the gardens of the hotel on a wooden bench and let my thoughts wander. I had wanted to ask him if he missed me or still loved me, or a thousand pointless questions, none of which, would ever be answered again.

There are things I would have liked to have said to him, such as that I now sleep on his side of the bed and wear his dressing gown. I really wanted to have told him, I wished I had stayed and fought the storms behind his eyes. Taken all his worries and hid them in my pocket. But the fire has turned to ashes and me to vodka and there was nothing I could do.

As the lights in the garden were turned off, I stumbled to our room and quietly ping-ponging off every bit of furniture I made it to the bed I now yearned for.

On shutting my eyes, they flew open from a sensation of not being alone. I looked over to his bed where he was snoring and sleeping soundly, so closed them once more. I crushed the smell of linen sheets between my palms and began to toss from side to side, the sensation of someone else in the room became stronger. Once more my eyes flew open. This time I saw him.

A man was sat in the corner of the room. As I stared at him, I noticed he had no eyelids and was sitting there without breathing. I asked him if he was really there not breathing and he nodded his assent.

Terrified, I edged out of the side of my bed and went over to where my husband was sleeping. I could not wake him up, no matter how much I tried to shake him awake, he was dead to the world. I looked at the ghost in the corner of the room, a face like all the forgotten faces who only had eyes for me. I wrapped my arms around myself to try to control my fear. Once my heartbeat was under control, I asked him, "What do you want?"

He ignored my question and told me to close my eyes, yet not one syllable did he utter. Ignoring his demand, I went over to the window, opened it and lit a cigarette. Aware of the no smoking laws in this country, I prayed nobody would be outside.

I watched the night slide by flooding the sky with my clouds. Evening was now imprisoned in cold jagged corners and I shivered from the cold. But like a child who does not want to go to bed and fights with all her might to keep her eyes open, I open the vodka once more and willed myself to stay awake. Once or twice, I checked behind me to see if the man was still there sitting in the same position and not breathing, he was.

I had no doubt that the presence sat in the corner of the room was a Trinket man.

The more vodka I drank, the more courage I had to engage in conversation with him. I say conversation but when you only hear replies without a mouth moving it is disturbing. But the vodka began to overcome that. I asked him when he had first appeared to my husband. He told me that it was over twenty years ago and that he had not just appeared, my husband had invited him in.

I was incredulous at that and I told him I did not believe him; my husband was ill and now I am here sharing his fantasies. He asked me if I thought he was a fantasy, and I barked back, yes of course you are! Without you and your stupid eyelids my husband might still be here. He told me I was wrong, I told him I was drunk and that this was just a stupid conversation with an illusion.

A door somewhere flapped like an angry flag in the wind, so I finished my glass of vodka and ignoring the Trinket man, I climbed back into bed. I could feel the rise of my heartbeats but stayed determined not to close my eyes. I looked over to my husband's bed and saw that his eyelids were fluttering. He was changing his imagery and concepts whilst dreaming.

Entering now the forgotten hours I struggled not to curl up and close my eyes. But as the music of breathing disappeared, I found myself behind the curtain of reality.

The Trinket man's eyes now in which I travelled showed me the road signs to take. The world had shifted and I listened for the footsteps of my dreams. From a distance, a voice whispered to me, this is you, wake up, as through some trap door in my mind I fell.

There is an absence of light here that colours things awake tapping the glass of my dreams. I want the dream to return to colours for this terrifies me. I want to scream, yet cannot. I notice that my shadow has left me alone in the darkness. I try to turn around and find myself entering the library of dreams.

How did I know this was the library of dreams if I had not been here before? Shadows were cutting into corners where the light was trying to hide. Sitting between myself and what is not me, I noticed that I was not breathing just like the Trinket man.

The silence fell around me like dust, my eyes were far away gleaming under closed eyelids. I saw shelves upon shelves filled with thousands upon thousands of dreams, the bubbles shivering in a false light. Tiny bubbles of memories shimmering, calling to my heart to choose one of them.

The feather-light fingers of ghosts began to talk to me about the forgotten scattered shards of my life. I received each piece of information and tried to put them together. Seeds were being born out of the jigsaw as I walked amongst the shelves. A shower of incandescent sparks burst out of the memories, snapshots of my past.

143

Placing one of the bubbles between my fingers, I hear the inaudible and set the bubble back on the shelf. Nothing I see here migrates to my heart, just the cold eyes of a fake angel. Facing memories, long ago smothered under the snow of her heart

Out of the world's reach, I asked the question, where did you go, my love, when the clock stopped?

I am injured by his absent presence, living a multitude of twisted days, a simple thread of dead thought. A solitary tear falls as a pearl onto my hand and I sigh, the deepest longest sigh. I cannot fix a broken shadow; can you hear me whisper I love you?

Suddenly, I see the Trinket man from the corner of my eye. He is sat behind the reception desk watching me check out one of the bubbles. I asked him if it was possible from here to cross over to another person's dreams.

He answered without his lips moving that I would have to cross through the mirrors. He told me that it was not what you dream but what it silences, so everything appears not as it seems.

I asked him to show me how to cross through the mirrors but he told me that I was not yet awake. He told me that as the light happens inside the eye, so the dream connects to the images of the day and goes back to the shelves to learn. I needed to learn to be awake even when I was asleep.

So, to the shelves I returned, selecting my bubbles at random.

Whispers of fireflies light the garden's flowers. A grey sky shivered as the seagulls cried to the wind. My old Westie, wrapped liked a pullover around my feet, snuggling ever closer. My angel, playing the flute, my baby girl strumming the strings of a guitar. The sweet juices of peaches and oranges dribbles down our naked bodies. The weather forecast says snow for tomorrow, searching for coal and a carrot.

Christingle, treasure hunts, fairy houses, diamonds, playgrounds, family shows, parties, Sunday lunches, blockbuster movies, laughter in the home, and a smiley face of happiness

Backgammon in the solitude of the sand dunes, always champion. A baby sparrow, risking his first flight in the rain trembles over the water. On your headphones you listen to Santana, black magic woman.

Heartache shadows of a place I belonged far beyond my call.

Inside the twisted spiral subtle code of my life, I see a brief mercurial flash of infinity. Sitting between what is and what is not. Where ever changing energy re-configures time upon invisible wires.

Still asleep inside my sleep, I hear a door close softly, I look over to the reception desk and notice the Trinket man has disappeared. I wondered if he had gone to make us a cup of tea, then giggled to myself at the absurdity.

Within the depths I had found myself, I began to think that we may all have Trinket men. Though everyone, may not, perceive them in the same way. They may be the smile in the unknown distance or the ones who startle the stars at night. The sounds of voices that whisper in the rivers. The flickering darkness inside a log's flame or the dark corner that swallows your shadow.

Transparent men, that pass through the crowds, or in between the lines of the page of books, giving to us their ideas.

The hours are vanishing now, swirling toward tomorrow. I am still drifting with my passport to roam these halls but I no longer have the passion to stay here and view the bubbles. As I was leaving, on one of the shelves a small bubble blinked at me constantly, clutching it between my fingers it was a memory that I could not recall. We were walking along clifftops and he picked up a shell. Holding the shell to his ear, he said there was a message in the shell, we descended to a beach and the bubble burst.

I walked toward the elevator and pondered over that which was hidden from me tonight. The trap had been laid, whatever I needed to learn, I now had to find.

This time I ascend in the elevator alone. Pressing a button to my left the pillow's edge appeared. I looked at the time on my watch and saw it was the dead hour. Climbing out of bed I drained the last dregs of my glass.

Finding myself now from my hiding place, I wondered if everything was just the dreams of a vodka addled brain, or was I still asleep inside his sleep?

His Voice

"So, I wait for you like a lonely house till you will see me again and live in me. Till then my windows ache."
– Pablo Neruda

When I woke up that morning, I knew there had been a change. Going down to breakfast she seemed in deep thought. I wondered if it was a hangover or if something had happened last night.

She asked me what the Trinket men looked like but I did not answer. Was she setting another trap or was this a genuine search for my knowledge? If I opened up and told her what they were really like, would an ambulance or the police draw up outside the hotel and take me away? She was not going to get rid of me so easily.

So, we sat in silence over bacon and eggs as she began to understand my obstinacy on the conversation. I wanted her to talk but there was no way at this time I was going to open up.

Sensing her annoyance, I tried to think of things to take her mind off the subject. What I needed from her was a promise that this time together, that we were sharing, would not end up with her calling for the police or ambulance.

So, I asked her to unclose her mind and just let things happen. I asked her to take down her barriers and just for once, believe in me. Even if what you think is not real, believe in me so we can find ourselves.

She nodded her acquiescence and I asked her what she would like to do with the day.

It was at this point she astounded me by saying she would like to visit the Library of Dreams.

I swallowed hard and asked her what she was talking about? she looked quizzically at me, but said nothing more.

I said that I would like to go for a long walk and would she accompany me.

This was not easy, we had this construct between us now where she knew I was lying, but we were caught between all that was and all that must be, and I did not want to spoil that.

So, trying to make amends I told her that if you believe something that has happened, whatever that may be, that is your mind. I don't want to question you on anything, just for now let it be.

I looked at the beautiful face in front of me soften and thought to myself that I just wanted her happiness back.

We went outside to smoke our cigarettes and stood by the wall where we declared our love. So much had happened in between that time. Could I really convince her to think we had a purpose? We were such different people now, our lives suspended on days without end.

How can we live beyond the now or travel back in time to obliterate the haunting shadow of the past? We are both trapped inside mangled clockwork with the hands spinning furiously both getting lost in profound pockets of sadness. Wrapping ourselves in ever coiling labyrinths, we are blind to the future.

We are now handicapped by all that is past and in the complexities of our lives we stagnate, swamped by all that is behind us. We are strangled by the joy and happiness of the past that now smothers us. I want us now to step from the dark and make things bright, to come awake in the infinite dream.

If I told her that I would spy on her in her new land would she believe me? Of course, not she would think I was crazy as normal.

I told her that I would like this time together to talk freely and without either of us being afraid. I wanted her to trust in me, but I did not want to go back to hospital. There is no help for someone like me in hospital, nobody thinks, like I think.

For instance, if I told you I was right at the end of an endless road, you would say that was impossible. But it is perfectly possible from my point of view. I can be everywhere, nowhere and somewhere at the same time. I was awake in the infinite dream, now I needed her to wake up.

I asked if we could make a pact where we open up to each other and accept or question each other's words without fear.

She agreed so off we set off on our walk. As we walked, I kept seeing the man who was not there but I dared not tell her. The next time I do not see him, I will not stare, just let my thoughts drift. Messages from him are seeping into me, but I ignore him.

After about ten minutes of our walk, I ask her if she has noticed anything unusual. She replied that she cannot believe how much everything has changed from our last visit there.

I know from her conversation that there is a something she has experienced now hidden in her heart. The experience has returned from a wild night within her and is nestling behind her eyelashes soundlessly.

This is now about trust; do we trust each other enough to open up or will our secrets continue?

Whilst we were on our walk, I picked up a shell and held it to my ear. A Trinket man began to whisper to me.

He asked me to take her to the next clifftop and descend to the beach. There was no way that I would question him on his request. So, when we arrived at the next clifftop, I asked her if she would come with me to the beach below.

She looked at me slightly shocked. I asked her if there was a problem, she answered that she had seen me in a dream last night do exactly the same thing. Then she nodded her assent and we began to descend the steep path onto the golden beach.

Once upon the sand, I picked up another shell. The Trinket man asked me to me to take her into the water. I asked him why? But I received no response. The waves were crashing upon the beach leaving a froth like an automatic washing machine upon the shore.

She was kicking her shoes off straight away and paddling near to the waves breaking. I stood one step behind not wanting to lose control.

I watched as she bounced forwards and backwards trying to escape the breaking waves. Holding up another shell to my ear the Trinket man said you need to wake her up. We cannot help you with her accepting everything just as it is. You need to force her into reality as she is not there yet.

A fear came over me, I knew what he was asking of me, and I could not ignore the voice that had taught me so much.

I took off my shoes and left them by the shore then followed her to paddle in the water. She turned and flashed her brightest smile at me as she saw my feet getting wet. My toes curled up in the freezing water and I shivered, not just from the cold. Holding out her hand for me to grasp it, we began to jump over the waves together. She was screaming with delight as we were dragged and then soaked each time on the ever-changing sea and sand.

Each time I looked at the happiness in her face, I began to doubt my Trinket man. But above the roar of the waves, he was insistent, you know what you must do, wake her up!

Just then an enormous wave came crashing towards us and stumbling I dragged her down with me under the wave. Her hand struggled to let go of mine, but I would not let go, I continued to hold her under the water. As the wave passed, we came up for air, then once again I moved us into the deeper water.

At this point her smile had now gone, I wondered if she was now aware that today was the end of all her dark days. I continued dragging her now faltering steps out to sea, after this there will be thorns and dark waters and then light.

When the next big wave came, I held her tight and plunged us beneath the sea once more. She tried to scream and struggle with all her might but it was useless, I was by far the dominant force.

She needed to wake up to what was reality for me, needed to show her the way. Once I felt her go limp under my grasp, I began to make my way back to shore. I began spelling out prayers as I dragged her body onto the sand. As the waves pounded onto the shore, I watched the water's foam along the secret line of her spine.

All the time I was wondering, was it enough, had she seen the light, how crazy would she be thinking I am at this point? As I dropped her onto the sand, the rain started to spring clean the Earth.

She was staring with her eyes closed, deep inside me, calling me a fucking crazy bastard. Ignoring her words, the Trinket men were calling out to me to wake her up. As they cried to me to choose an end, I just looked at that dear face beneath me.

Suddenly I had become the silent assassin with an open scream for a smile. The sea roared and the skies above closed ominously.

Holding my face up to the rain, and as if drowning now myself in thundering water falls, I pressed my lips to hers and breathed.

Immediately she gasped, then choked, then punched me in the face as hard as she could.

Your 'what the fuck' was the most pleasant sound I had heard, along the lines of when you told me you loved me, and when you said, "I do."

As the breath entered into you fully, there was a no hold barred diatribe of swear words, in between the words you just tried to fucking kill me!

Now I was shocked, not in one instant had I wanted to kill her, all I had wanted was for her to see my reality.

After a few more punches and a few more fuck you's, she grabbed her shoes and left.

And then there she was walking away from me, always the same view of the back of her head, and as the wind had a conversation with the waves, she left me alone on the beach.

His Voice

"Don't walk behind me; I may not lead. Don't walk in front of me; I may not follow. Just walk beside me and be my friend."
– Albert Camus

When I entered the room at the hotel, she was packing. Her usual stomping around the room, angry type of packing. A sort of packing with the certainty that she had to go, type of packing. This was not a messing about type of packing, I understood that.

I only want to love you for eternity I said, she ignored me. Please let me explain my actions I said. She ignored me. I crashed her suitcase to the floor, she ignored me. I went over to where she was stomping, she hit me.

Rubbing my face, I said you told me that you would accept my actions without fear and now here we are with you running for your life. Please calm down, just stay and let me help you understand my actions.

"I did not let you die, did I?"

For the first time I saw her face soften.

"I am who I am without any choice in the matter and you are you without any choice of how you respond to me. I have such a desire to show you things that you think are crazy, if you no longer care what I think, I would believe that you did not love me anymore.

"Do you remember when I used to jump out in front of traffic? That was not me trying to commit suicide, I was trying to wake the motorists up to reality. There they were on their commute to work or wherever, on automatic pilot listening to the radio or thinking about the day ahead.

All I was trying to get them to do was see that this was not reality. Also, when I said the building was moving, it may not have been moving for you, but your reality is not mine. When I set off all the fire alarms in the hotel, this was because I needed to wake the world up and let them see my reality.

"I need you to know that when I held you under the water, it was not my intent to drown you. It was to wake you up to my reality. One of the Trinket men had asked me to do this, so I followed his instruction, I believed that it would wake you up to my world, never to kill you."

For the first time her anger got the better of her again.

"So, the fucking voices in your head tell you to drown me and you believe them? This is why you are so dangerous to be around, this is why I had to leave you and go to another country. And here you are off your medication and listening to voices again!

"You know that if I called your team now and told them what you are saying, you would go straight back to the unit?"

I replied that of course I knew that but then I asked her if she had seen a Trinket man?

Her face once more changed and I knew my thoughts were correct that a Trinket man had been to visit her.

Her answer though was one I did not expect, she told me she was drunk and it was all a dream as I had fed her mind with so much information about the Trinket men.

"I imagined him just as you told me he would look, without eyelids, not breathing, a man who is not there. And that is the thing when you really, really, think about it, and I mean think really hard, he is not there!"

I had no idea what to say, as this was nothing that I would have expected. What I needed now was a Trinket man to show up in front of both of us.

I gently picked up her suitcase from the floor and began unpacking her things.

"You are going nowhere," I said. "Until we sort this out. Hold onto the fact that I did not let you die and that I love you. If you believe in this then we will work this out. Come with me now, walk beside me, and be my friend, please."

Taking her hand in mine I walked out of the hotel and back to the wall. Pinning her back up against the wall, I kissed her deeply.

She tried to squirm out of my hold, but our lips had connected and I could feel her melt one more time into my arms. Within seconds she pushed me off, glaring at me, she told me do not to do that again. But hope now filled my heart again as I had felt her melt.

So just taking her by the hand, I walked her to a local café for lunch. She still would not talk to me but as I ordered her favourite, a baked potato with prawns, I noticed a certain light come back into her eyes.

The café had relaxing music coming through the speakers, so we sat in silence listening to some soothing piano music that was playing in the background.

I told her that she was not going anywhere and that we needed to work things out.

Her sarcastic reply was to say, what like two crazy people?

Her Voice

"The most dangerous liars are those who think they are telling the truth."

Did you seriously believe the last chapter, do you not know yet what a delusional liar he is? Someone who believes one minute he is Jesus; the next he has alien visitors.

I have learnt from the past not to believe a word he says, he lies.

His delusions told him to kill me, so he tried. So why am I now, still sitting with him, appeasing him into thinking that everything is OK. To be quite honest I am scared of him, but as I have told you I have an enquiring mind and I want to understand how this has happened to us, I also just simply love him.

After lunch we went to visit an aquarium, I wanted to be amongst other people, dive into a blue fantasy. Forget what had just passed between us and watch rainbow coloured fish lazily passing through the seaweed's long green hair. The vista creating a dreamlike meadow where silver ribbons waltz on beds of coral.

My love for him was not the size of the oceans, no not that size, it was infinite.

After the aquarium we went for fish and chips and sat on a bench once more overlooking the ocean. The salty, vinegary, deliciousness, of that simple meal was one I always pined for when I was abroad.

Long ago I had realised that without each other we were nothing but dust. Time is relentless, marching us always away from our birth, its blueprint lying in the beat of our hearts.

As we crumpled our chip wrappers into the nearest bins, we lit our cigarettes and began to walk back to the hotel.

With my tummy full, and my confidence returned, I asked him about what he had done, did he truly believe that I would suddenly see the light?

He said that he believed that I had actually seen a Trinket man and that I was not being truthful with him when I told him it was a drunken delusion.

So, I said to him, that what he did today was under the influence of the Trinket man and that he must see that he nearly killed me. I believe what would be best for us both is if we rid ourselves of the Trinket man. If he was no longer talking to the Trinket men, but only to me, we could work this out. But the Trinket man was dangerous and we needed to confront him and get him out of our lives.

He told me that beyond my walls was another life beyond the mind. He had already left that world behind. He said he saw me as drowning already deep within an illusion and I was not alive.

All he had wanted to do was gather himself into a hurricane and shake me into wanting to be alive like he was. He said that once I had survived the hurricane, I would never be the same.

How tempting were his soft words, like a mystic he played on a sense inside me that this was not all there is. So, I asked him if he we could try to meet with a Trinket man in person, so that we could ask him questions together, then see if we could get rid of him so we could change our world back to normal.

He told me that we could try but was not sure if it would work. He added that he did not know their rules or if it was even possible for two people to see them at the same time.

We decided to return to the hotel and try to contact the Trinket man that night. I asked him how he usually made contact but he did not know. They would only come to him when they were ready, not the other way around.

I felt fluttering in my stomach that evening, I really would love proof that he was not insane and that all he had been telling me was the truth after all.

But all the fine minds of science had told me that he was completely crazy. He had a condition called schizo-affective disorder and that there was no cure.

When we were back in the hotel room, I asked him if we should sit a special way, as if in meditation. Should we light candles, say prayers?

He laughed and said we don't do anything, if he comes, he comes. So, he turned on the TV and began to watch football. I lay on my bed staring at the ceiling, willing the Trinket man to appear.

I imagined him now, the man who wasn't there, with no eyelids. I willed him to come back and talk to us. But I know I do not have the freedom to call him, it is not my choice.

He is sitting behind several doors to oblivion and his spider's web has extended beyond freedom. He does not care, that tonight, I want to call out to him, he has already decided how he will respond. I have nowhere to hide from him after all. He has always been inside my mirror watching me as I brush my hair and clean my teeth. He listens silently to the beats of my body and if I were to whisper my rebellion, he would relish the fact that I know nothing. For he is arrogant in his ways and demands payment in trinkets.

I asked my husband if he thought the Trinket men were evil, as the tasks that he made him do were quite dangerous.

He replied that he thought they were here to try to teach him something so huge and important for the world that it would obviously include danger. I asked him if he had any trinkets with him that we could give him if he came.

He told me that he had taken one of my beads off my Pandora bracelet and that should suffice. I looked at my wrist and sure enough a small silver starfish was missing.

So, we sat and waited and then waited some more. I rolled around on the bed from my back to my stomach, back to my back once more. My husband just sat watching the football seemingly unconcerned with what we were waiting for. Sighing and cursing at each miss of his team's ball.

At some point in the night, I must have fallen asleep, not sure whether front or back but awoke on my side the following day.

His Voice

"Sooner or later a false belief bumps up against solid reality."
– George Orwell

She thought I was watching the football, but I wasn't, a Trinket man had been whispering in my ear for the last hour of the match.

The referee blew his whistle a couple of times at me to pay attention. But I ignored him and listened to what the Trinket man was telling me.

He told me that the next day he would come in disguise, so as not to look out of place amongst the ordinary people we would meet and that I was to go on a road trip with him and my wife. We would get my wife to take us to some caves nearby and he would impart some lessons to us.

After the match had finished, I noticed that my wife was now asleep. So switched the TV off and went to bed, feeling that tomorrow could be a good day as it may finally answer her question as to whether the Trinket man really exists or not.

The following morning, I told her that a Trinket man had spoken to me. She looked confused and asked me why I did not wake her up. I told her that he had not appeared and we were just conversing as we usually do. She looked at me unconvincingly but brightened when I asked her if she would like to go on a road trip.

After breakfast we left in the car and she asked me where we were heading. I did not want to tell her that I did not have a clue. So, I decided to choose a route from the map I was staring at which took us along the coast road to other towns. Even if we did not meet the Trinket man at least it was going to be a pretty ride.

So, we set off with a packed lunch that we had asked the hotel to make for us, and as the wind blew down the road going nowhere, so did we.

She slid our CD of the Gypsy Kings into the player, and as she beat the rhythms to her steering wheel, I did flamenco with my feet on the floor.

Ahead, I saw a young man with braided long hair holding out his thumb for a lift. A whisper in my ear told me this was our man.

I asked her to pull over and give the hitch-hiker a lift. She replied that it may be dangerous to stop and give a stranger a lift. I countered with that we were not children anymore and told her that I thought it may be a Trinket man.

Astonished she asked me why.

I told her of my conversation last night, and to believe that this was a Trinket man, but he was in disguise.

She slowly pulled over to the side of the road and the hitchhiker gave us a huge bow of his head with his hands clasped together in prayer. His smile lit up the car and he asked us where we were going.

To this I quickly questioned where would you like to be dropped off? He told us that he wanted to visit the Dolaucothi gold mines and was it on our way.

I replied that it was such a coincidence as we were going there ourselves. My wife cast me a look but I ignored it.

She switched the music off and made conversation with the young man. He was from Sweden but spoke very good English. He had been backpacking around Europe for over a year and loved visiting caves and mines. As soon as he mentioned caves, I knew this was him, this was our Trinket man in disguise.

We drove on along the coastal road from Fishguard and stopped at Newport for a coffee. There was one thing about the Swede he never stopped talking. I was starting to think he was using his disguise too well. But I had to go with the signs and he wanted to see the gold mine which was an entrance to a cave. This is what the Trinket man had told me, soooooo......

After we had finished our coffee, we went back to the car and now all introductions and small talk had been made, we drove on to the gold mine in silence.

I tried tuning in to him to see if he would let his disguise slip and show me a way, but no, he just sat in the back of the car watching the road.

Once we arrived at the mine, within the most beautiful nature you ever saw, we parked just outside the entrance and discovered the mine was closed throughout the winter.

My wife asked us both what we should do now and I asked the Swede if he wanted us to take him somewhere else. As I suspected he said no, why didn't we get ourselves some supplies and camp there for the night he suggested.

My wife looked aghast at sleeping under the stars but we both managed to convince her it would be fun. Luckily for us all, the Swede had come prepared with a multitude of things to help make us comfortable for a night under the stars. My wife went off in the car to the nearest town to buy food, we could cook on a campfire, also vodka and beer. We were going to have a party!

As it was not warm, my wife brought back sleeping bags for her and myself also, the Swede was fully kitted out with whatever he needed.

With daylight full of hours before the curtains drew, we set up our little camp and the Swede made us a campfire.

Which never on Earth could my wife and I have produced. We had never led the back-packing life of our contemporaries; we were always to be busy working.

My wife had brought back sausages, hot dog buns, marshmallows, crisps, peanuts and drinks. She explained to me it was the only food she could think of for camping and cooking.

The Swede accepted her offerings gratefully and opened up a beer, passed me one, then lay back on his sleeping bag.

"When are you two going to start talking?" my wife asked.

I am just waiting for the right moment, I finished my beer and opened another, the cool frothy bitterness quenching my thirst.

As night drew in, the Swede asked us if we wanted a smoke?

We both said yes please at once, as smoking was still one of our pleasures.

The swede then brought out from his rucksack a little tin box. my wife and I were used to filtered cigarettes brought in supermarkets. I quickly offered him one of my mine from my packet, but he shook his head.

"No," he said, "I'm going to make us all a spliff."

My wife had never tried one. But I guessed that the Trinket man wanted to open her mind up, so we watched him roll this enormous joint full of green and brown stuff. He lit it then inhaled deeply and passed it to my wife, my wife also inhaled deeply then passed it to me.

I took a pull on the spliff and passed it back to the Trinket man. As the drug entered into my system, I noticed no change. We continued to pass the joint around between us, until all of a sudden, we burst into uncontrollable laughter. I was laughing harder than I had in years, yet there had been no words uttered.

It was the most delightful feeling I had experienced in a long time. If all mental health drugs that were given made us feel like this, the patients would take them all the time.

The seconds like hours passed by our eyes and the colours of the stars came into view.

Pinpricks of cracked ice appeared glittering, watching me, as I watched the starlight pulse and vibrate, dark knots of matter twisting and turning the Milky Way.

At last, I spoke and asked the Trinket man why he had decided to come with us today.

He replied that he was not sure, he needed to get to A to B, and his adventures always took him by surprise. He supposed he could ask the same question and say why did you pick me up.

I told him that he had arranged for me to pick him up, somewhere along the coastal road. He gave me a quizzical look, then said yeah cool. You are going for an every-thing is connected vibe, yes, I understand, I had arranged for you to pick me up in my thoughts when I needed to get to the mines. Yeah, I get that totally. Cool, man.

I told him that all night we had been throwing words to each other but that the words were now floating along a stream. Nothing that had been said was enlightening me as to why he was here.

I took out of my pocket my Trinket from her Pandora bracelet and handed it to him. He looked at the little silver shell and tears came to his eyes.

"Aww, guys, you did not need to give me anything, it is really kind of you both."

So, I said, presents now exchanged, can we drop the disguise and tell her everything you know so that she will wake up to my reality?

"Hey guys, not sure about your reality, but my philosophy is just to go with the flow. Don't get stressed or worry about the small stuff, life is for living, loving and peace and all that other bullshit!"

I was starting to get angry with him. He was supposed to show his hand now. Not give a hippy diatribe on love and peace and how wondrous the world was.

He heard the change in my tone and smiled.

"Listen dude, not sure what you want me to say right now. Just chill, enjoy the smoke and the stars, and relax."

I looked over to my wife who was listening, but not listening, to our conversation. She giggled now and then, but she did not appear to be interested. Her attention had been drawn to a blade of grass and she was studying the blade as if she would a road map.

I could not believe that my Trinket man would let me down so spectacularly once again.

So, I tried to conjure others to help me. Nobody was forthcoming I drew a blank. My mind had been clouded by the weed. I had no clarity.

I decided to lie on my sleeping bag and watch the stars. I sat now amongst their whispers with eyes on the skies. Thoughts and imaginings rolled like waves inside of me. Gleaming webs of conspiracy now spiralled around me. Irrational visions and superstitions gather in my thoughts. My new budding thoughts are now becoming the strangest flower.

Within the prison that was my imagination now stirs creative lights. The debris of my thoughts, now past, sit on derelict building sights. I am awakening to the idea the Trinket man is no more real than me.

Suddenly all the carved etchings of my brain are there, unzipped, waiting, ready for my perusal. Ideas now sparkling with absolutes, not maybes.

He is my Trinket man, someone who wants to know my thoughts and actions, who wants to wake me up, he has planned this all along.

I sat straight up from my position and challenged him.

"I want you to show me your true self now."

The Swede looked at me as if I was delusional.

"Ok, what would you like to know?"

I responded that I wanted to know about reality and show my wife what we talked about, not this bullshit drippy hippy talk you have been talking.

He smiled and said that life was what you make it, reality is an illusion and that you need to go inside to find yourself and your reality.

I answered that what if inside yourself was damaged, how could you be sure you were seeing reality and not a diseased brain?

Do you know what he did, he laughed!

He laughed in my face, when I was ultimately serious, wanting a serious response to a serious question he laughed. I thought of how this person had nearly killed my wife and I became white with anger.

Beyond the volcanic red of lava, this man in front of me was responsible for me being in hospitals for over fifteen years. Believing in him had nearly drowned the woman I loved. Looking at him now in human form I detested every single atom of his being.

By the side of me was a rock, I clenched it in my hand, I looked over to where my wife was now lay, she had succumbed to sleep.

I asked the Swede/Trinket man if we could continue our conversation elsewhere so as not to disturb her.

He acquiesced so we began to walk through the fields. I asked him again about reality.

He responded, "Hey, man, why are you going so deep? Just let the smoke drift into your brain, there is no need to go so deep."

He lit up another spliff and took a toke, then offered it to me. As I was inhaling, another Trinket man came to me.

"What are you doing with the rock?" he asked.

I looked at the rock in my hand not realising that it was still wedged there.

"I will ask you once more what are you doing with the rock?"

I looked at my hand, every movement was making time move forward, the past and future now the same distance away. Staring into his eyes I am aware that we can both see the same.

I no longer see myself, so turn around to try to find me. I am long gone, some part of me has gone back to the camp fire staring at my wife sleeping.

I watch from a distance as a glove covers my hand of stone, my mind fixated on the guidance of the man who is not there.

I watch the blood drizzle then ooze into the earth. Astonished how the earth claims the blood for its own.

I hear sounds like fingernails upon a chalkboard, but ignore them, the Trinket man has perfected his painting, never to be stored in my memory.

I am now gently floating along the fields as a soft breeze now wrinkles a moonlit pool. The moon hangs like a fresh Emmental, and as I breathe the cool air I relax and fall asleep next to my wife, who is gently snoring.

Her Voice

"The eye sees only what the mind is prepared to comprehend."
– Robertson Davies

Waking the next morning I saw that my husband was asleep but the Swede was missing.

I decided to light the fire once again and use the left-over sausages with the eggs I brought for breakfast. As they were slowly cooking, I walked out into the fields to stretch my legs. It was there that I encountered the Swede's body lying in a pool of blood. It looked as though he had fallen during the night and smashed his head on one of the rocks nearby.

I ran over to him and checked his pulse; he was not breathing. I wanted to scream but held my breath.

Running back to the campfire I woke my husband up.

"Please you have to come quickly the Swede has had an accident."

He woke drowsily but then realised the urgency in my voice. As we neared the body, my husband started to vomit.

We both looked upon the young man's body and shuddered.

"He must have woken during the night stoned, gone to relieve himself, and fell and hit his head," I said.

My husband said that we must leave immediately, I looked at him quizzically, surely, we must call the police and ambulance and tell them what has happened.

But he was adamant, there was nothing we could do, "Let's get out of here now". He said.

At once I understood the situation, did you have something to do with this I asked?

From the look he gave me I knew he had.

He was the Trinket man he said. You have always told me that they are a part of my delusions and not real. Everything that happened yesterday told me that the man, you think is never there, was finally there in front of us. He asked me to kill you, so I decided to kill him, now he has gone from our lives. You told me that you wanted to be rid of him to make our lives better?

I flopped down onto the ground and held my head in my hands trying to take in what he had just told me. Then I remembered the library of dreams where I picked up the bubble of a shell whispering into my husband's ear.

He was right, the Trinket man needed to be destroyed for us to be free, and if I trusted in my husband, he had actually enabled this.

Believe me, he said, I was not killing a person, I was trying to kill the man who was not there. The person who directed me to wake you up, his eyes beseeched mine to believe him.

And I did.

What I had no idea of was, what to do next.

My husband had killed what he thought was a Trinket man, and now a real-life body lay on the ground in front of us. Yet I had no idea if this was a man backpacking his way through Europe?

I wanted to scream, get angry with him, erase the day, cry for the young life that was lost. But I did none of those things. Let's pack up and go now I said.

We both could not eat, so I extinguished the fire and threw the remains of the now burnt breakfast into a rubbish sack. Loading up all our belongings into the car we headed off towards Snowdonia. Just before we left, I saw him go back to the Swede's body.

"What on earth are you doing?" I asked.

He offered me back my trinket from my Pandora bracelet.

"The Trinket man has gone now and this is yours to keep," he said. "He did not deserve to keep this trinket."

I sighed, yet slipped it back onto my bracelet. I now felt we were part of a Hollywood movie; we were on the run.

"How does it feel to kill someone?" I asked him.

"I cannot remember it," he replied.

"But you told me this morning you had done it?"

"Yes, I remember seeing the blood," he replied, "I think there was a Trinket man there but cannot remember much else. I think the Trinket man took care of the rest of it."

Should I be frightened at this point? Should I take him straight to the police station? How much do I love him?

What I decided to do next, many will disagree with, but as I see it life, is but the waiting room for death. We are born into a hospice waiting for our turn to die.

We have no choice in this, as soon as we have submitted ourselves to accepting life, we are sitting in the waiting room of death. This may come quickly or last over a hundred years, not one of us knows when the shooter will come. His spider's web extends beyond freedom, there is no choice. Your fragile thread remains attached, he does not care that you have forgotten you are the one. He loves when his bullets only play with your hair and you draw the duvet over yourself to hide your pain from the world. He is arrogant in his ways, knowing one day that you will scream for him. And if you die an ordinary death, just surrender before he shoots you, for he is a specialist, there is no need for thought.

But for now, we were heading for the mountains, like Thelma and Louise, our film had begun. How long could we last before the body caught up with us was another matter. But for now, we were on our way.

But I am frightened, he has now shown once again that he cannot distinguish between what is and what is not reality.

The clock is ticking.
Past grows, future decreases.
Worries are mounting.

His Voice

"I shall look at you out of the corner of my eye, and you will say nothing. Words are the source of misunderstandings."
– Antoine de Saint-Exupéry

The photographs in my mind are disappearing, moving away to the land of the absurd. As the moon, and the night, and the blood, dissolve I forget the faces.

The landscape splits into ago, and today, I hold my head in my hands to forget the echoes. As the past sinks back into the depths of the shadows, I feel I am unravelling.

I feel like I am travelling through rapids, and your island is becoming more distant and remote. As though your music is on the strings of a guitar and I am vibrating on a sitar. Out of tune now, are notes are not the same, you are so far away from me. How do we navigate these troubled waters?

I dare not tell her. If I even breathed that I was unravelling, she would open window after window to tell everyone of my downfall. I try to climb the string of language that connects me to the world but find I do not have the alphabet to tell her what is going on now inside me.

I try to muster the right words into my mouth to calm her but my dictionary is now suspended in time. I ache to tell her the truth but my mind just whispers in the breeze from the tops of the mountains. My body is now sheltered by the wind.

We booked in to a hotel that night in a place called Betws-y-Coed. I had no idea how to pronounce it but apparently there is a waterfall there.

We both sat in the bedroom on the end of our beds not talking. She seemed angry, whilst I was numb, I told her that I should sleep. She got out her vodka and poured herself a large glass.

I laid my head onto the pillow but sleep sat in the station with the usual delays. Under the heaviness of eyelids and thick night, I breathed in, breathed out, breathed in, breathed out, wondering what we were going to do now.

Her Voice

"Things do not change; we change."
– Henry David Thoreau

I downed my Vodka quickly and poured myself another. Lighting a cigarette, I went and opened the window and sat staring into the black night.

I knew he wasn't sleeping, but I knew I could not go to sleep whilst he was awake, for he terrified me. I am now trapped inside some mangled clockwork, the hands spinning out of control and I am lost in profound pockets of fear.

What are we going to do?

Last night had changed everything and our lives were never going to be the same again.

Everything that we did not understand has made us what we are today. Time is like nothing, yet time is like always and we had no time to waste, we had to decide what we were going to do next.

I knew it would not be long before the Trinket man's body was discovered and people would remember us. At the coffee shop on the High Street there was probably some CCTV footage of us all leaving and getting in the car together. Also, my trip to the supermarket, to buy our food and sleeping bags, all must have been captured. The hotel where we stayed would say, we did not stay for the entire booking. So many things now were whirling through my head. Once thing was for sure we could not stay in Wales.

That is when I came up with a sort of plan to get us both out of the country before we were being chased out.

It felt like I was entering into ever coiling labyrinths, lost in the now, blind to the future. But I had to choose a path and quickly. For the time being I needed to suspend today, for it is always today and I am always me. We needed a new direction.

Finishing the dregs in my glass and pouring another it suddenly hit me, he had actually killed someone. This was not in his head anymore, this had entered real, or had it?

The whole of yesterday is now falling out of my grasp, I can no longer comprehend the situation we are in. The vodka is addling my brain and I just want to listen to music and sing. Go back to smoking a spliff and watching the universe turn through the night.

Just as I am rising to get my phone, I see the man who is not there. My eyes did not know what to say, I was taken back at my deceit in thinking he was now gone from us. Staring at my error I sink onto the bed shaking my head.

"What the fuck are you doing showing up?" I asked him.

"My husband just killed you."

Except it wasn't exactly the person my husband killed, as this man in front of me was not there. Oh, how I wish he would go away and leave us alone. As before, he just sat there not breathing, this time though with something akin to kindness in his strange eyes. Maybe the vodka was softening my thoughts against the would-be assassin.

I went over to the bed and shook my husband to wake him up.

"Wake up Goddamit! The person you killed is in the room right now!"

But there was nothing, he just rolled onto his side and let out a snore.

After about five minutes of me screaming for him to wake up and shaking him, I gave up.

So, I turned my attention to the man who was not there.

"Why did you kill the Swede?" I asked

"I have never killed anybody," he answered. "How could I, for in your mind I do not exist. How can you kill someone if they do not exist?"

An echo of me says you do not exist; you are mere wind ruffling my feathers. But when I close my eyes, I can still feel your gaze. How can this be so?

"Are you a figment of my imagination now, like you are his?"

"I do not even know what a figment of the imagination is," he replied.

"All I know is that you are very real to my husband and you have now made him do despicable acts."

"Despicable to whom?" The Trinket man answered with lips unmoving.

"Well, obviously, that poor boy that we picked up today thinking he was you."

"Your petty fears and worries and sympathy for someone you did not know, tells me you have learnt nothing."

"Stop it, what do you mean I have learnt nothing, there is nothing you could say that would make me feel better."

"I will ask you a question," the Trinket man said. "What did you do when you saw that body today? I will tell you what you did absolutely nothing. You just tried to protect your husband, nothing more and nothing less. You did not call an ambulance; you did not call the police. No, you told him to get out of there lickety-split."

He made me dumbstruck with his reply, for it was true. I had not done one thing to alter the situation, I just wanted out. It was too uncomfortable for me to have stayed there and answer questions. I could not stand the thoughts of hours at a police station, eventually the hospital. I did not want to stop my understanding of my husband's reality.

"What you are saying is true?" I told him.

"So, stop fighting me," he replied.

"Where do we go from here?" I asked.

"Believe in fate or free will, believe this is your husband's life, just as this is your life. Let him be free to believe in what he believes in."

"But if what he believes in destroys other lives, how can I stand by and let this happen?"

The Trinket man answered, "You have your own fate and free will. You decide whether to call the police or not. Now we are talking about your life, which is completely separate to his life. You make your decisions on your own. He will counteract with his decisions. But know these are your decisions and yours alone. You cannot live another person's life; you can only live yours."

It was now a fundamental choice for me, a life on the run, or call the police.

Where did I want to be, living dangerously with him or apart once more with a hole inside of me, living and breathing like a polo mint? There is no lightness of being in this story, every decision weighs so heavily upon the soul.

As a single metaphor can give birth to love, we constantly walk in to our memory of better days. Our past so full of energy and life and our future this apathetic void.

I am still wondering how we got this far, my husband's two minds, unaligned, different. One side is barbed with an electric fence, the other side viewing the world so innocently.

Only I could make the decision of what we should do next. Either I accept the delusions and continue or I do not accept the damaged mind sleeping next to me.

Would he think I had betrayed him? Yes.

But looking back at history which should teach us what we need to know, he always thought I betrayed him.

So, what difference would one more betrayal make? None, which is why, I decided to do the opposite.

Before we left the town, we visited the waterfall. Whispers of ice shuddered down my spine as we watched the never-ending cascade of water falling over the rocks and into the pool below. As l on the outside constructed reality-based dreams, I on the inside, sat on an invisible wire dancing over the waterfall.

Watching the water with the moon in my throat, I wanted to leap the world's net. Dive into the cascading water, and ask myself, where to now shall we float?

Her Voice

"I want you always to remember me. Will you remember that I existed, and that I stood next to you here like this?"
– Haruki Murakami

I guess you now know, what decision I made, I booked the next flight from Manchester airport to leave for 'paradise'.

Sat inside my head I wondered how it would work out, as there would be no medication there for him, I would have to wing it.

I knew he was unravelling, but how on earth could I leave him?

The following morning when we awoke, I told him to pack his things he was coming home with me.

At first, he looked confused, are we going back to my home or yours? I told him we were going back to the land of his birth.

Straight away he began to pack, there was no need for words it was where we needed to go.

Once on the plane he asked me about the Swede. I told him not to worry he had killed the right Trinket man. Once we landed in the country of his birth, we both relaxed. We were now in our homeland.

The only blight on the landscape I could see was his illness was getting worse and this was definitely not the land of magic cures.

I checked out the English TV but as yet nobody was saying anything about a dead body being found at the Dolcauthi mines. Crossing my fingers that the Swede's body, would lay undiscovered until the mines opened, I relaxed.

As the days vanished, swirling into strings of tomorrow, our faces and bodies altered with stresses and time. The more I heard nothing from the TV, the more I believed it was our Trinket man whom had died.

The world continued to sing her alien song but at last with him beside me, I did not feel so disconnected. My only problem was I was walking now with a shadow. There were no more normal conversations, once more reality had flown out of the window.

The wind once more sang through my empty vodka bottles as I watched all boundaries dissolve into the air.

It has become a full-blown opera where angels soar, Devils mounting their backs. Light playing chess with the dark as to who has the upper hand.

So, in these transparent complexities of life, we stagnate. Swamped by all that is between us, and strangled, by the reality that smothers us.

As the months turned into summer and still no word of a body I began to relax.

The Trinket men left us alone, and I was so happy that even though he was ill, he truly believed he had killed them in his head.

That was when the cancer struck out of the blue, it may have been so long on the injections who can say. But it struck and struck hard within two months of sensing something wrong we had a terminal diagnosis.

So now from my perspective, and all that had passed us by, I accepted his death.

In the mirror it was a Tuesday and the hands of summer had gathered ripened fruits. With his eyes now full of hours, we listened to the wind's sweet flutes. Clouds gathered overhead until darkness spilt its black silk.

The words fell like tears into our hearts, for there was nothing left to say on the day there was so much to say. So, we sat waiting for the midnight hour as his breathing slowly disappeared. The stars still shone in his eyes and caught my heart but within one of us, the life had gone.

And as the music of breathing disappeared, I separated into two minds, pain free.

At first, I tried so hard to find him again, I kept calling his name in the mirror, writing his name in the mist of the bathroom. Drenched in a hundred blue dreams I would stagger to the mirror each day only to make the outline of his name still there.

Sometimes heart racing, I would worry without reason and stare out the window just waiting for him to open the front gate.

An echo of me, told me he no longer existed he was merely the breeze ruffling the flowers.

Other times I would carry my vodka bottle to sit on a moon edged roof on a warm summer night pining away from loneliness and wishing for hugs. Remembering once, that I and the world had colour, I look for him in everything but he does not exist anymore.

When I close my eyes, I can feel his gaze, my solitude an absence of his echoes. The hope of ever seeing his smile again turned the hours into thieves.

One night as the light was being slowly dusted from the sky, I stepped into the corridor of my house. You were staring with your eyes closed deep inside me. As my answer machine beeped and took my calls, I heard your voice, softly, it called my name. As if I was drowning in thundering waterfalls, I saw that the two doors each end of the corridor stood open. A voice called out to me to choose an end. As I approached one door, it slammed shut, then teasing and barring me the opposite door did the same.

Blue shadows began to stalk my footfall, as the door handles began to shiver with invisible hands, the walls suddenly broke into infinity, and there I saw you always walking away from me. Always the same image, of the back of your head, and as the wind has a conversation with the shadows, the walls closed bringing me back to the dead.

Her Voice

"Time is not a road - it is a room."
– John Fowles

When the knock on the door finally came, I was not surprised. They took me to one of the local police stations here and asked me questions.

But to be honest by that time I was simply trying to learn how to stop breathing. I summoned now a Trinket man at will. You were always now behind the mirror simply waiting for me.

I sit now in a cushioned room, in some place or other, taking tablets and being looked after. I told the police the absolute truth as I have written it down for you.

My statement is there for anyone to read, my husband thought he had killed a Trinket man and I believed him. I had spoken to the Trinket man the very next day but he would not confirm or deny my story as the man was not there. I told them that I knew how difficult this must be for them to understand but it was the truth.

After so many questions someone else was brought into the room with a gentler touch.

I explained again and again to them what had happened. I believed that the person my husband killed was a Trinket man and I wanted to bring him back to the land of his birth to get better.

But you see, don't you, I was not quite telling the truth as I had serious doubts whether or not it was a Swede or a Trinket man. I just thought it was an easier story to tell than that I was in doubt, for I would have been an accomplice.

Well, the upshot of that was I was passed into the mental health system with a psychotic disorder. Apparently I had a folie a deux. Or a madness Shared by two, or a shared delusional disorder, what does it matter the name.

Oh, how my husband would have relished this now, after all the years of me thinking he was crazy.

And so, because I decided to try not breathing at all, I am now in the cushioned room with the clock on the wall, wondering my escape through the mirrors.

I try to call my Trinket man from here, but just silence, must be the tablets. Then again he never once came if I asked!

I try when on the point of sleep going back into the Library of Dreams, nothing. I decided to fake taking the tablets, I had been so good so far. All they did was deaden my brain to not feel anything.

I was like a grey blank canvas.

Slowly, slowly, my mind began to awaken, until one night when being and not being are the same I followed my shadow along a bridge. A jigsaw of light puzzled on the floor and my steps became impatient.

Far off darkly before the bright exit stood someone I was waiting to meet. His features as usual were unrecognisable, yet my shadow cried out to greet him. As the unknown babbled back some clouded noise, I tried to grasp the voice.

When the wind began to change direction I was suddenly fearful of my choice. I am here to ask, for immortality, to splatter and split this universe apart. To discard once and for all illusion or delusion and enter reality.

As I approached the Trinket man I noted that my shadow had vanished. I was left alone to see everything.

The Trinket man asked me if I had left anything behind that would torment itself and yearn for me. Was I willing to enter a land I had never seen and cease to understand what I thought was reality?

I wanted the gift that immortality would bring.

I nodded fast, there was now no decision to be made, and then there he was as I crashed through the mirror. Climbing inside me he turned his face; I immediately understood and returned his call.

So, we sit together once more in the room where all is told, with a clock playing lento with time, knowing that time does not exist.

He is wearing cream chinos, an open neck blue linen shirt and sandals. I am wearing the grey pencil skirt and emerald green blouse. These were the clothes we wore when we first met.

At last I understood, I was awake, the clock's hands were moving backwards, and this was the beginning of the end.

When the nurses opened the padded cell the next day, they saw the woman who was not there, all that was left in the room was a book of scribblings, on top was a note, saying, I leave it to others to make their own minds up.

This was our truth, and one day we will return, we will, just not yet.

The End of The Beginning